Books by Ed Dunlop

The Terrestria Chronicles
The Sword, the Ring, and the Parchment
The Quest for Seven Castles
The Search for Everyman
The Crown of Kuros
The Dragon's Egg
The Golden Lamps
The Great War

Tales from Terrestria
The Quest for Thunder Mountain
The Golden Dagger
Return of the Dagger
The Isle of Dragons

Jed Cartwright Adventure Series
The Dangerous Journey
The Lost Gold Mine
The Comanche Raiders
The Lighthouse Mystery
The Desperate Slave
The Midnight Rustlers

The Young Refugees Series
Escape to Liechtenstein
The Search for the Silver Eagle
The Incredible Rescues

Sherlock Jones Detective Series
Sherlock Jones and the Assassination Plot
Sherlock Jones and the Willoughby Bank Robbery
Sherlock Jones and the Missing Diamond
Sherlock Jones and the Phantom Airplane
Sherlock Jones and the Hidden Coins
Sherlock Jones and the Odyssey Mystery

The 1,000-Mile Journey

Tales from Terrestria:

Book Three

A sequel to The Golden Dagger
by Ed Dunlop

cross & crown
PUBLISHING
RINGGOLD, GEORGIA

©2010 Ed Dunlop All rights reserved

www.talesofcastles.com
Cover Art by Rebecca Douglas

Return of the Dagger: an allegory / by Ed Dunlop.
Dunlop, Ed.
[Ringgold, Ga.] : Cross and Crown Publishing, c2009
199 p. ; 22 cm.
Tales from Terrestria Bk. 3
Dewey Call # 813.54
ISBN 978-0-9817728-8-2
0-9817728-8-9

When sixteen-year-old Prince Eristan becomes the king of Cheswold, opposition arises from an unexpected source, and the result could be the destruction of Cheswold. Determined to save the kingdom, the young king stands firm against the enemy until his sister Cordelia is kidnapped.

Dunlop, Ed.
Middle ages juvenile fiction.
Christian life juvenile fiction.
Allegories.
Fantasy

Printed and bound in the United States of America

That my King would give me the heart of a servant.

*And whosoever will be chief among you,
let him be your servant*

— *Matthew 20:27*

Chapter One

The full moon glided across a cloudy sky, a silver ghost of a ship sailing a stormy sea. Still, its brilliant beams couldn't seem to penetrate the inky darkness of the forest. A cold wind swept in from the north, snarling and vicious. Save for the angry voice of the wind, the forest was silent. Not a creature stirred. Danger lurked in the shadows, an evil so intense that the trees themselves stood stiff with terror.

Eristan ran desperately down the narrow forest trail. His lungs burned and his legs throbbed with pain, yet he dared not slow his pace, even for an instant. The terror that pursued him was hardly a dozen paces behind him, and gaining every second. As he ran, heart pounding as if it would burst, he could hear the heavy footfalls and the harsh, heavy breathing that told him he was about to be overtaken.

In his terror, he glanced behind him, but could see nothing. He turned back just in time to see the dark silhouette lying across the trail, but it was too late. The fallen log swept his legs from beneath him and he tumbled headlong to land face-first in a carpet of leaves. Drawing his knees beneath him, he rolled to one side of the trail and ended up beneath a dense thicket. He heard the sound of a heavy body striking the log, followed by a grunt of pain and the crunching of autumn leaves as his pursuer tumbled after him.

Eristan held his breath, waiting, listening, but heard nothing. Taking a slow, trembling breath as quietly as possible, he turned his head and scanned the darkness. After a moment he could make out the shadowy form of his pursuer lying facedown on the trail. A flash of moonlight glinted on the huge blade of the weapon intended for him, and he shuddered in horror. Still on his knees, he took several slow, deep breaths and then began to crawl noiselessly through the thicket.

On the far side of the thicket, six or eight paces from his assailant, he quietly rose to his feet and listened intently. The forest was still and all was quiet. He took a deep, trembling breath, let it out slowly, and carefully crept through the thick undergrowth. His heart pounded furiously and he trembled in every limb, but perhaps he would make it, after all! He could hear no sounds from the man who had pursued him so relentlessly. Moments later he came to the trail, and a thrilling sense of relief swept over him as he hurried back down it. He had eluded his pursuer.

"I have you, lad!" With a roar of vicious laughter, a tall figure leaped into the path, brandishing the fearsome weapon. Eristan saw a flash of silver moonlight glinting on the sharp blade. His heart constricted with terror and his legs gave way as he fell to his knees in the middle of the trail.

"Did you really think you could escape me, lad? You fool!" The tall man threw back his head and roared with laughter. "You should never have attempted to run from me, lad, for now I shall deal with you even more harshly!" He seized the collar of Eristan's tunic with one hand, twisting it until the youth cried out in pain, and raised the gleaming weapon with the other hand.

"Nay!" Eristan screamed, twisting free of the man's fierce grip and rolling to his feet in one motion. Plunging through the tangles of the undergrowth, he ran frantically through the darkness, heedless of the branches and briars that tore at his face and clothing. He ran until his feet became lead and he could run no more. Collapsing on the forest floor, he gasped for air.

His heart constricted in terror as a steely hand seized his shoulder. "Give it up, lad!" a cruel voice demanded, and the hand jerked him to his feet. "There's no use running—you'll never escape me!"

A silver beam illuminated the man's thin face, and Eristan looked up into cruel eyes that glittered with hatred. Snarling, the man drew Eristan close until his face was mere inches from his own. "Where's your sister?"

"I-I don't know, s-sir," Eristan stammered.

The man shook him furiously. "I'll ask again, lad, and I want an answer this time! Where is your sister?"

"I-I don't know."

Gripping Eristan's tunic with his left hand, the man raised the sharp weapon.

"Garven!" Eristan screamed. "Garven, don't! Please, sir, I beg you—don't! Garven, don't, I beg you!"

"Dathan, wake up!"

Garven shook Eristan's shoulder. "Wake up, lad, or I'll make you wish you had!"

Eristan stiffened and tried to pull away.

"Dathan, wake up! It's all right. Wake up! You're dreaming, Dathan—uh, Eristan. Wake up."

Eristan slowly opened his eyes. He was flat on his back and a flickering flame hovered just above his cheek. Beyond the amber glow of the flame he could see the face of Cordelia, his twin sister.

"You were dreaming, Eristan. Everything is all right."

Eristan took a deep breath, shook his head as if to clear the terrifying images from his mind, and then sat up. "Thanks, Cordelia. That was one of the worst ones yet."

"It was Garven again, wasn't it?"

Eristan nodded. "I dreamed he was chasing me with a haying sickle."

His sister touched his cheek in a tender gesture. "Garven can't hurt us now, Eristan. You're the king of Cheswold, and he's just a stablemaster."

Still half asleep, Eristan looked around the tent to make sure that the cruel stablemaster was not present. Cordelia hovered over him with an ornate lamp in her hand. He took a deep breath. "I'm not the king yet."

"Aye, but next month you will be. You can make Garven lick your boots."

Eristan laughed at the idea. "I know that Garven can't touch us now, but I still feel cold chills every time I think of him. He was so cruel, Lanna—uh, Cordelia."

Cordelia smiled. "We're both having trouble with our new names, aren't we?"

Her brother nodded. "I have a hard time thinking of myself as the crown prince of Cheswold, and I still haven't gotten used to the idea of you being the long-lost Princess Cordelia." He shook his head. "I still think of myself as a commoner, a lowly slave, and the thought of seeing Garven again brings fear."

She nodded. "Lord Keidric says that we'll reach Windstone Castle just before sundown tomorrow. Garven will stand before you then. I can't wait to see his face when he learns that you are his king, not a lowly goatherd."

Eristan was silent.

"Your Highness," a deep voice sounded from outside the tent, "is all well?"

"Aye, all is well," Eristan assured the guard, without opening the tent flap. "I was awakened by a troubling dream, that's all."

"Call me if you need anything, sire," the knight's voice replied. "May Your Highness enjoy pleasant dreams for the rest of the night."

"Thank you, Captain," Eristan replied.

"What are you going to do to him?" Cordelia asked.

"The captain?" Eristan frowned. "Why would I do anything to the captain?"

"Nay, not the captain, silly," the girl said with a laugh. "What are you going to do to Garven?"

"Well, first of all, choose your words carefully when address your king," Eristan replied. "Use the word *silly* again and I can have your head taken off."

"You wouldn't!"

"If the situation calls for it, I would," her brother replied, struggling to keep a straight face and a stern look.

"You wouldn't execute your own sister!" Cordelia studied his face. "Would you?" For an instant, a look of panic swept across her features and Eristan knew that he had her.

He maintained the fierce countenance for another few seconds and then laughed as he hugged her. "Of course not, Cordelia," he assured her. "But you had better be very nice to me."

She laughed with him. "Aye, Your Majesty," she said stiffly, raising one hand in mock salute. "I'll be as sweet as honey on bread."

Abruptly, the twins were convulsed in laughter. "I haven't gotten used to the idea of you being the king of Cheswold," Cordelia giggled. "I've always known you as a commoner,

Dathan the goatherd, and now you're to be King Eristan? My mind still struggles with the idea."

"Not that it's any easier for me to think of myself as King Eristan," her brother replied. "I also think of myself as Dathan the goatherd. Who would have ever guessed that you and I are the long-lost prince and princess of Cheswold?"

"So what are you going to do to Garven when you see him tomorrow?" Cordelia asked again.

Eristan frowned. "I'm not sure," he replied slowly.

"He was awfully cruel to us," she reminded him. "He hated us." A look of delight swept across her face. "This is your chance to make him pay for all the mean things he did to us."

The young prince was thoughtful. "I'm not sure what I'll do when we see him," he told her. "I guess I haven't given it much thought."

"Well, I have," she declared fiercely. "Have you forgotten all the times he kicked me and hit me, or the times he punched you? Have you forgotten the nights when he sent us to the hayloft without supper? Have you forgotten the time he pushed me face down in the manure, or the time when he lied to Lord Keidric and had us flogged?"

Eristan was silent.

"I hate him, Eristan, and believe me when I say that you need to make the most of this chance to get revenge. If you can't think of anything to do to him, I have some good ideas."

"I'm sure you do."

Cordelia kissed Eristan on the cheek. "Well, good night, Your Majesty. Get some sleep. And if Garven shows up in another nightmare, just remind him that you're the future king of Cheswold! That will put some fear into him." She stood and grinned at him. "I can't wait to see his face when he learns who you and I really are! My, is he going to regret what he did to us!"

With these words, she slipped from the tent and disappeared into the darkness of the night. Prince Eristan knelt beside his pallet, removed a small parchment from within the pages of a book, and began to write a petition to King Emmanuel. In his petition, the young prince asked for guidance in his meeting with Garven, and also for wisdom in handling the affairs of the kingdom.

"Your Majesty, I am but a youth," he concluded, "and hardly qualified to govern the kingdom of Cheswold. I humbly ask that you would grant me wisdom beyond my years that I might rule in justice and integrity. May I honor you in my decisions. Your son, Prince Eristan." He rolled the parchment tightly and released it, watching in satisfaction as it disappeared through the fabric of the tent. Moments later, he slept peacefully.

Windstone Castle swept into view as the cavalcade of Windstone knights topped a rise. Lord Keidric raised one hand and the knights drew their powerful steeds to a standstill. Eristan stood in the stirrups, gazing intently at the distant castle, and a cold chill swept over him as a myriad of painful memories surfaced.

A tall nobleman on a handsome black stallion reined in close to him. "Things are different this time, Son," Reginald of Orwyn said softly, for he read the young prince's thoughts. "You're visiting Windstone Castle as the crown prince of Cheswold. Garven will fall on his face before you."

Eristan nodded. "I know, Pa," he replied quietly, "but this feeling of fear comes over me every time I think about him."

Sir Reginald smiled. "That's natural, I suppose. The man was very cruel to you and Lanna."

"Cordelia."

Sir Reginald laughed. "Aye, Cordelia. I, of all people, should have no problem with your true names, for I knew them all along."

Lord Keidric wheeled his horse alongside Eristan's. "Welcome to Windstone Castle, my lord. My castle is yours and my people are at your service."

Eristan nodded once. "Thank you, sire." He grinned. "Perchance the hospitality will be better than last time."

The nobleman bowed his head in contrition. "I ask your forgiveness, my lord. My people did not know your true identity."

Eristan laughed. "For that matter, neither did we." He studied the castle for a moment and just then an idea struck him. "Cordelia and I will wait here. You and your men take our horses and ride into the castle without us. Have one of your men bring us two peasant cloaks to cover our regal clothing. Garven thinks of us as slaves, and that's how he will see us. I want to see his reaction when he learns our true identities."

"Aye, Your Majesty." Lord Keidric turned. "Sir Reginald, if you would, sire, remain with the prince and princess."

Reginald nodded. "As you wish, sire."

Eristan and Cordelia dismounted. Two knights rode forward and took the reins of their horses, and the cavalcade of knights rode toward the castle. Moments later one knight returned with two worn cloaks, which he handed down to Eristan and Cordelia.

The twins donned the garments. Cordelia turned to her brother. "How do I look?"

"Like a peasant, except for your hair."

"Aye, I forgot." The princess unpinned her hair, allowing it to cascade down around her shoulders. She ran her fingers through her tresses and shook out her curls.

Eristan's heart was pounding as he and his sister hurried toward the castle. When they reached the drawbridge, they both paused for an instant. "Welcome to Windstone Castle, my fair sister," Eristan said in a low voice. "This time, things will be vastly different."

The twins crossed the drawbridge, passed through the main gates and the barbican, and entered the bailey. The courtyard was filled with castle residents who had gathered to watch as Lord Keidric and the Windstone knights returned. The knights had dismounted and servants were tending to their horses. The stablemaster, Garven, was leading Lord Keidric's horse toward the stables when he caught sight of the twins.

"Here," the stablemaster snarled, handing the reins to a servant. His face was a mask of fury as he strode briskly toward Eristan. "Where have you been, you cur dog?" he growled in a low voice. Trembling with rage, he reached for Eristan.

The young prince allowed the cloak to fall open at that instant, revealing his regal garments. Garven gasped, and his head jerked back as if he had been punched. His eyes bulged. "Garven," Lord Keidric called in a stern voice, "bow before your king!"

The stablemaster's face turned pasty white and he trembled uncontrollably. "Sire," he replied, and his voice cracked, "I don't understand."

"On your knees, man," Lord Keidric commanded. "The prince who stands before you is the next king of Cheswold!" The tall stablemaster collapsed. Moaning in terror, he lay on the ground before Prince Eristan, quivering and terrified.

Lord Keidric lifted his voice and addressed the castle residents. "Today, my people, the future of Cheswold unfolds before you!"

A chatter of excitement swept across the crowd.

"As many of you know," Sir Keidric continued in a loud voice, "fourteen years ago the Karnivans invaded Cheswold and besieged Barrington Castle. King William was killed in the ensuing battle and the crown jewels were stolen. The king's own son and daughter, barely two years old at the time, disappeared mysteriously and no one has heard from them since. Until now!"

Sir Keidric paused for effect and slowly scanned the crowd. "Today you stand in the presence of Prince Eristan, the long-lost prince and future king of Cheswold, and Princess Cordelia, long-lost princess of Cheswold!"

An audible gasp went up from the castle residents. Stupefied, they stood staring for several long seconds, and then, as one, they fell to their knees and bowed their heads.

"Prince Eristan and Princess Cordelia recently lived among us as commoners and we did not know their true identities," the nobleman continued. "We treated them as slaves, and for that we beg their forgiveness and their mercy." He fell to his knees before the twins. "My lord and my lady, can you find it in your hearts to forgive us?"

"All except Garven," Cordelia declared fiercely. "He must pay for his cruelty to us."

The terrified stablemaster trembled as he awaited the inevitable.

Chapter Two

As the residents of Windstone Castle looked on in stunned silence, Prince Eristan stepped over to the prostrate figure on the ground. Quivering and moaning, Garven lay face down. "I beg you, spare my life," he pleaded. "I ask for mercy, for I had no idea that you were royalty."

"Royalty has nothing to do with it," Eristan replied sternly. "No person, whether peasant, nobility, or royalty, should ever receive such treatment as we received at your hands."

"It will never happen again, my lord," Garven pleaded. "I give you my word."

Watching the pathetic, quivering figure before him, Eristan felt a pang of sympathy, and for just an instant, considered extending mercy toward the cruel stablemaster. He glanced at his sister, and in that instant, memories came flooding back. He thought of the many beatings that he and Cordelia had endured. The harsh words. The relentless abuse. As old memories surfaced, his heart hardened. The man deserved no mercy.

And then, for a long moment, the young prince hesitated. Kind and gentle by nature, he had no real desire to inflict pain upon another human being. Cordelia slipped beside him.

"Remember the time he pushed my face into the manure?" she asked softly. "Remember the times we missed supper? Think of all the times he made us keep working when all the other servants had quit for the night. Think of all the times he gave us the dirtiest jobs, just to be cruel to us. Make him pay, Eristan, make him pay for every cruelty."

A flash of anger surged through Eristan's soul. "On your feet, wretch," he growled in a low voice, and his own words brought a sadistic sense of pleasure. Garven had inflicted many a wound, and payback would be sweet. Trembling uncontrollably, Garven stood with bowed head. His face was ashen.

"To the stables," Eristan ordered.

"Aye, my lord," Garven replied quietly, and immediately headed in the proper direction.

Upon reaching the stables, Eristan ordered the stablemaster to go behind the building where the pigs were kept. "In with the swine," he ordered, and watched as the trembling man climbed over the fence into the pigsty, stepping into ankle-deep muck. "Kneel down," he ordered, and Garven did.

Eristan turned to two male servants who watched from a distance. "Get two carriage whips and flog him until he passes out." The men's eyes grew wide, but they moved obediently toward the tack room.

"Eristan," a low voice said sharply, and the young prince turned to find Sir Reginald at his elbow. "Sire, may I remind you that you are not a commoner now. Don't conduct yourself as one."

"What do you mean, Pa?"

"You are soon to be the king of Cheswold. You and Cordelia are royalty, the son and daughter of King William himself. As the crown prince, you now have the power to inflict incredible suffering upon this man, but you must remember that you did not come to the kingdom to serve yourself or to avenge yourself for any personal injuries or slights. The throne is not given to you so that you may fulfill any personal desires; it is given you so that you may serve others."

Eristan was silent.

"A commoner would seize this opportunity to exact revenge upon his enemies," Sir Reginald continued, "but you are no commoner. You are royalty, and soon to be the king of Cheswold. How would a king conduct himself in this matter?"

The young prince shrugged. "I must say that I do not know."

"As the king of Cheswold, you will derive your power and authority from King Emmanuel himself, for he rules all of Terrestria, and thus, in reality, you serve him. You must therefore learn to emulate him. How would he respond to Garven at this moment?"

Eristan hesitated, for though he knew the answer, he did not wish to say the words.

"His Majesty would never exact revenge upon such a man as Garven," Sir Reginald continued, "for that is not his royal nature. As you study Terrestrian history, and in particular, the history of Emmanuel, you find that he forgave any and all who came to him. Not once did he seek revenge upon those who wronged him. Even those knights who abused him before his execution found him willing to forgive, though they had done their worst to him."

"You said that King Emmanuel forgave all who came to him," Eristan countered. "Garven has not asked my forgiveness nor sought my pardon."

"You have not given him that opportunity," Reginald replied.

The two servants stood in the pigsty with Garven, looking to Prince Eristan for orders. The young prince took a deep breath as he thought the matter through. The stablemaster had not only tormented and humiliated him, but also had abused Eristan's sister. Forgiving Garven's wrongs against him would be one thing, but forgiving him for Cordelia's sake would be a different matter entirely.

Eristan released his breath in a long sigh. "I can't forgive him, Pa. You don't know what he did to us, what he did to Cordelia. He was brutal, Pa."

"The Judan knights were brutal to His Majesty, yet he forgave them willingly. If you seek to follow Emmanuel, as you must if you would rule Cheswold properly, you must do the same."

The young prince was silent as he studied Garven's face for several long moments. There was no animosity or defiance in the stablemaster's eyes, just fear, and . . . At that moment, Eristan saw something else. The man's countenance displayed an attitude of submission. He was willing to recognize Eristan as his king and submit to his authority.

With bowed head and eyes on the ground, Garven spoke for the first time. "Do what you will with me, Your Majesty, for I was intentionally cruel to you and your sister and I deserve the worst. But please know that I am sorry, truly sorry, for what I did. When I was a very young boy, a youth about your age killed my older brother. Every time I saw you, I thought of the killer, and I'm afraid that I took my grief and anger out on you. Your Majesty, no matter what you choose to do to me, please forgive me for what I have done to you and the princess."

Eristan couldn't speak.

"What would Emmanuel have you do, Son?" Reginald asked quietly.

The young prince was torn. One part of him longed to forgive the man who knelt before him, while another part wanted to see him suffer for what he had done. Memories of the cruelties inflicted by Garven flooded in again at that moment and Eristan felt irrepressible anger surging within his soul. He wanted revenge and it was now within his power to make the cruel stablemaster suffer.

But he also wanted to become the very best king that he could possibly be, and to do so he would have to follow King Emmanuel. And that meant forgiving and releasing Garven. For several long moments the battle raged deep within his soul. Sir Reginald and Princess Cordelia stood quietly, knowing that the decision would have to be his alone.

At that moment a beautiful white dove soared across the courtyard on motionless wings and alighted in the top of a sycamore. Eristan's heart ached as he followed the flight of the celestial bird. He knew what he had to do. At last, he spoke. "Release him. It is my desire to follow His Majesty, King Emmanuel. Garven, you are forgiven."

A look of relief swept across the man's face. "I thank you, Your Majesty," he said quietly, with head bowed. "I do not deserve this kindness."

"Forgive me for even considering the idea of making you suffer," Eristan replied. "You may go in peace." As the young prince walked back to Cordelia and Sir Reginald, his heart was at peace, for he knew that he had done the right thing.

The cavalcade of Windstone knights rode hard as they escorted Lord Keidric's elegant coach down the winding country road. Inside the coach, Lord Keidric, Lord Stephen, and Sir Reginald sat facing the twins. Sterling, the youth who had accompanied Eristan and Cordelia on their flight to Ainranon, sat beside them. "We should reach Barrington Castle within the hour," Lord Keidric remarked, "though this weather doesn't look good." He glanced out the coach window and eyed the darkening skies. "We could be in for a blizzard."

At that moment the clouds began to spit snow, and within minutes, the air was filled with huge white flakes. The north wind began to howl, driving the snowflakes in tight, swirling circles and making it difficult for the coach driver to see the road. The temperature dropped rapidly.

"I can't wait to see Vladimir's face when he learns of Prince Eristan's claim to the throne," Lord Stephen remarked. "He'll drop his teeth."

"Vladimir has enjoyed the throne," Sir Reginald replied. "This will come as quite a shock, I'm sure."

"Will he resist?" Eristan asked. "Will he try to keep the throne?"

"I don't think so," Sir Reginald answered. "He knew when he took the throne that it was a temporary position, that he was merely a regent, and that you would become the king of Cheswold on your sixteenth birthday. He knows as well as anyone that your birthday takes place in two weeks."

"But he doesn't even suspect that I'm alive," Eristan stated. "I doubt if he's expecting to relinquish the throne."

"True, Vladimir doesn't yet know that you are still alive, but he knew when he became regent that he would have to relinquish it one day."

"Aye," Eristan argued, "but when you took us into hiding, it was as if we vanished from the face of Terrestria. For fourteen long years, no one but you even knew where we were or that we were still alive."

"I know it will come as something of a shock to King Vladimir," Lord Keidric offered, speaking loudly to be heard above the voice of the wind, "but I'm sure the transition of power will be a smooth one. We'll meet with Vladimir's court and cabinet to work out all the details and assist you in the selection of your own cabinet of advisors, and I'm certain that Vladimir and his men will help in every way they can."

"One of the first things you'll want to do, Your Majesty," Lord Stephen told Eristan, "is to review the troops and determine the strengths and weaknesses of the army of Cheswold. We know that Grimlor and the Karnivans are planning an invasion of Cheswold, and they may try to take advantage of the transition as the time to invade. Cheswold must be ready."

"Aye, sir," Eristan replied. "Then we must look to the security of the southern border in particular."

The three men nodded in agreement with Eristan's statement. "Indeed we shall, sire," Keidric replied. "The security of the border must become one of the first priorities."

"How long is the border?" the young prince asked.

"The eastern half is formed by the great river gorge," Keidric answered, "and it's rugged and impassable. Grimlor's armies could not attempt to cross there. The western half would be approximately ninety miles long. If Grimlor attempts an invasion, that's where it would take place. Somehow, we must guard that border against a surprise invasion."

"What if we were to construct a fence along the border," Prince Eristan suggested. "Just a simple barricade of logs, maybe ten or twelve feet high, with two strands of iron wire above it. We could also build watchtowers every mile or so, just close enough that each tower would be in sight of the next one. The towers could communicate via a system of flags by day and torches by night. The barricade would not keep Karnivan raiders out, but it would keep them from sneaking in, for we would know if the wall was breached at any time. Word could be passed along the border within minutes and riders could be dispatched to warn Barrington Castle."

"Brilliant," Lord Stephen said quietly. "Simple, but effective. Prince Eristan is already thinking like a king."

"Such a system would be effective on clear days," Lord Keidric observed, "but not on foggy or rainy days when visibility is poor."

"We would also plan for riders to monitor the barricade on a daily basis," Prince Eristan told him. "If the wall was breached, we could track the invaders and attempt to overtake them before they attacked. At any rate, such a system would preclude a surprise attack upon Cheswold."

Sir Reginald nodded. "Excellent, Your Majesty, excellent. There will be a myriad of details to work out, of course, and the plan would not be completely foolproof, but I do believe that it would work."

Prince Eristan turned to Lord Stephen. "As you suggested, we will review the troops at once to determine the strengths of the army of Cheswold." He looked from one man to another. "Gentlemen, in what present condition do you suppose I might expect to find our army?"

Lord Keidric gave a long, noisy sigh. "I, for one, suspect that our forces are greatly lacking, both in training and equipment. I hope that I am wrong, but I suspect that Vladimir has been lax in that area."

"There are rumors that Vladimir is actually in league with Grimlor and the Karnivans," Lord Stephen commented, "and that he wants to merge Cheswold with Karniva."

"Emmanuel, help us," Sir Reginald replied.

Prince Eristan and the men continued to discuss plans and strategies for the defense of the kingdom for some time. Sterling glanced out the coach window and let out an exclamation. "Look! Is that Barrington Castle?"

The twins looked out the window. Just ahead stood a massive castle with immense walls and soaring towers. The royal blue pennants flying from the towers bore the image of a dragon and a sword. "Vladimir's coat of arms," Lord Stephen observed.

"King William's coat of arms was a lion and a crown," Sir Reginald said reverently. "Prince Eristan, that coat of arms now belongs to you."

"The castle is enormous," Sterling observed. "It must be ten times as large as Windstone!"

The cavalcade of Windstone knights followed the coach up the castle approach. The coach crossed the drawbridge and then slowed to a stop just as the horses reached the gatehouse. Behind the coach, the knights dismounted at the edge of the drawbridge. Lord Keidric stepped from the coach and approached the gatehouse.

A sentry met him. "What is your business, sire?"

"I am Lord Keidric of Windstone Castle," the tall nobleman replied, "and with me are Sir Reginald of Orwyn and Lord Stephen of Marden. We desire an audience with King Vladimir."

"His Majesty will not be disturbed today," the sentry replied curtly. "He is granting audiences to no one."

"Please inform His Majesty that we have an urgent message with a direct bearing on the future of the kingdom," Lord Keidric told him. "Our meeting with him will be the most important he has engaged this year."

"I would doubt that, sire," the sentry replied, with a note

of disdain in his voice. "And as I said, His Majesty will not be disturbed today."

"Please inform His Majesty that I bring a message from King William himself," Lord Keidric persisted.

"King William has been dead for nearly fourteen years, sire."

"Exactly. But I bear a communication from King William that was written on the very night that the king died. It's in reference to William's own son and daughter, the long-lost Prince Eristan and Princess Cordelia."

The sentry looked stunned. He eyed the coach for a long moment as if trying to determine a course of action. Finally, he summoned a second sentry. "Take this gentleman to stand before King Vladimir. He insists that his matter is of such urgency that he must see His Majesty today." He gave Lord Keidric a stern look. "I warn you, sire, that if your matter is not of utmost importance and you therefore arouse His Majesty's wrath, the consequences shall fall upon your own head."

Lord Keidric shrugged. "So be it."

The second sentry turned away. "Follow me, sire."

Lord Keidric didn't move. "My companions must come with me."

"You have permission to seek an audience before His Majesty alone, sire. I would advise you not to press the issue."

"My companions must come with me," Lord Keidric insisted. "Once King Vladimir learns the nature of my errand, he will demand to see all of us."

The sentries exchanged glances. "As you wish, sire," replied the first sentry. "But again, you are responsible for the consequences. And your knights stay where they are." He looked up at the driver. "Pull the coach into the barbican for the moment."

Having overheard the entire exchange, Prince Eristan opened the door of the coach. He glanced at Cordelia. "King Vladimir is about to learn that you and I are still alive."

Together Eristan and his entourage followed the sentry through the inner gate and entered a vast, elegant courtyard. Cordelia paused in utter astonishment. "Look at this!" she exclaimed. "Did you ever see such beauty? This is magnificent!"

Well-manicured lawns and exquisite flower gardens stretched as far as the eye could see. Fountains and statuary and groves of well-kept fruit trees added to the grandeur of the bailey. Nearly half a mile in the distance, on a promontory overlooking the rest of the castle, perched a magnificent palace with soaring towers and turrets.

The sentry led them up the steps and across the portico of a magnificent building of white marble. They passed through massive double doors that appeared to be fashioned from solid gold and then entered a vast anteroom brightened with colorful tapestries and elegant statuary. In the center of the room, a tall fountain of gleaming black marble soared nearly to the ceiling.

"What elegance!" Cordelia said softly. "Just think, Eristan, soon this will all be yours!"

The sentry gave her a strange look.

"The kingdom does not belong to Eristan," Sir Reginald told her quietly. "As king of Cheswold, he will serve the people of the kingdom."

The sentry looked from one visitor to another as if perplexed by their words. "Wait here," he told them, as they reached another set of ornate doors. "Perhaps His Majesty will deign to give you an audience."

He was gone for nearly ten minutes.

"This doesn't look good," Lord Keidric whispered to Lord

Stephen, but Eristan overheard him. "Surely he won't resist."

"His Majesty, King Vladimir, is extremely busy just now," the sentry announced, slipping back into the anteroom, "but he will see you for three minutes. He says that you are to state your business and be brief about it."

"We will be as brief as possible," Lord Keidric promised.

Prince Eristan's heart was pounding as he and his companions followed the sentry into a vast chamber with a gray marble floor and a frescoed ceiling. The walls were of teak and ivory and decorated with colorful standards. At the far end stood an enormous throne with six golden steps leading up to it, and upon the throne, a large, fierce-looking man with a thick, black beard. Three knights in colorful uniforms stood at attention on each side of the throne, while a number of richly-dressed courtiers sat along the outer walls.

"Your Majesty," the sentry announced, standing ten paces from the throne, "Keidric of Windstone desires an audience with you. With him are Reginald of Orwyn and Stephen of Marden, as well as three young people whose names I did not procure."

King Vladimir lifted one hand as a signal for the visitors to advance. As they stood before him, he studied the group in silence for several long moments. At last, he spoke. "State your business."

Lord Keidric bowed slightly. "Sire, I will be brief, though what I have to say is of utmost importance to the kingdom of Cheswold. As you will remember, nearly fourteen years have passed since the Karnivans invaded Cheswold and besieged Barrington Castle. You will remember that King William was killed in that battle and that the King's son and daughter, Prince Eristan and Princess Cordelia, were spirited away. You were inaugurated as regent the very next day after the

Karnivans were routed, and you were commissioned to occupy the throne until such a time as Prince Eristan would become king. According to Cheswoldian law, Prince Eristan is to take the throne of Cheswold upon his sixteenth birthday. As you know, sire, the birthday of the long-lost prince takes place within a fortnight."

"Sir, you bore me with your recitation of Cheswoldian history," King Vladimir interrupted, glaring at Lord Keidric. "Please state your purpose in appearing before me." He turned and eyed Prince Eristan suspiciously.

"Sire, I will come right to the point," Lord Keidric said boldly. "Before you today stands King William's own son, Prince Eristan, crown prince of Cheswold, and heir to the throne of his father."

Exclamations of astonishment swept across the assemblage of courtiers as all eyes darted to Prince Eristan. King Vladimir's head jerked back and his mouth fell open. He raised one trembling hand, started to speak, and then paused. Silence reigned in the throne room.

After several long moments, Vladimir recovered. Standing to his feet, he barked, "Preposterous! Imposters, every one of you!" He glared at Prince Eristan for several long seconds and then turned to his guards. "These imposters intend to seize the throne by treachery and subterfuge. I want them arrested at once and thrown into the dungeon."

Chapter Three

Prince Eristan and his companions stared at King Vladimir for several long seconds as the shock of his words sank in. Silence reigned in the throne room. Drawing their swords, the guards moved forward.

"Wait!" Sir Reginald demanded, raising one hand. "Sire, we can establish our identities beyond doubt and prove our claims beyond challenge." He turned to the group of magistrates seated to the right of the throne. "We have legal, documented proof of Prince Eristan's claim to the throne, as well as irrefutable proof of his identity. Under the jurisdiction of royal Cheswoldian law I demand that you examine these proofs and documents."

"Seize them," Vladimir snarled. "Arrest the lot of them and throw them into the dungeon. The integrity of the throne of Cheswold will not be compromised by this assemblage of imposters."

The guards moved forward and soon had Eristan and his companions in irons. "Come along quietly," the captain ordered in a low voice, "before His Majesty loses his temper and orders your execution." As the disconsolate group was led from the throne room, Eristan looked over his shoulder at

Vladimir and caught the distressed look that appeared upon the man's bearded face.

A cold, gray light stole across the dungeon as Prince Eristan yawned and stretched. The cell was tiny, hardly adequate for one prisoner, yet he was sharing it with Sterling and Sir Reginald. He sat on the floor with his back against the cell door, knees drawn up against his chest, toes touching Sterling's leg. Sir Reginald was stretched out beside Sterling.

Sterling stirred, rolled over, and then sat up. "How did you sleep in that position?" he asked Eristan.

The young prince shook his head. "I didn't. I've been awake all night trying to figure a way out of our predicament, and I've sent numerous petitions to King Emmanuel. I've come to the conclusion that King Vladimir intends to attempt to keep the throne. And if that's the case, it means that he intends to hold us as prisoners indefinitely."

"Or worse."

The young prince nodded. "Perhaps."

Sir Reginald sat up and stretched. "Did you get any sleep, my prince?"

Prince Eristan shook his head. "Pa, what are we going to do? I really think that King Vladimir intends to hold us here forever in order to keep me from the throne, and I see no way out."

Reginald grinned. "You once freed Sterling from the dungeon at Windstone Castle. Perhaps he can now free us."

Prince Eristan smiled sadly. "There's only one problem with that, Pa. Sterling's in here with us."

"Even if we do get out," Sterling commented, "how are we

going to establish that Eristan is the crown prince? We have no proof."

"Oh, we have proof all right," Sir Reginald replied. "It's just a matter of being given the opportunity to present it to Vladimir and the magistrates."

"What proof?" Sterling asked. "The golden dagger?"

Before Sir Reginald could reply, footsteps sounded in the dungeon corridor and the trio looked up to see two men approach the cell. The three prisoners stood to their feet as one man unlocked the door. The second man stepped into the cell.

"I trust that you passed the night without too much discomfort," he told them. "I regret that you have been treated in such a manner and hope that we can resolve this matter quickly." He looked at Prince Eristan. "If you are indeed the crown prince and your identity can be established so that you take the throne, I would ask that you would find it in your heart to be lenient and forgiving to the members of the court."

"Who are you, sire?" Prince Eristan asked.

"I am Lord Wallace, Chief Magistrate of Cheswold," the man replied. "This morning I risked my life by calling for an emergency meeting of the High Council. It took some doing, but I talked the other magistrates into demanding a second audience before King Vladimir, at which time you will present whatever evidence you possess as to your identity. If it can be proven that you are indeed Prince Eristan, son of King William and heir to the throne, then the High Council will force King Vladimir to abdicate."

He smiled. "The Council will meet in forty-five minutes. That will give us just enough time to feed you some breakfast and allow you to freshen up a bit. Again, I am sorry that you were forced to spend the night in such quarters."

"Where is my sister, Cordelia?" Prince Eristan asked.

"Please follow me," Lord Wallace replied pleasantly. "She and your other companions wait for you now."

The magistrate led them along the corridor and up a flight of stairs. As they reached the top of the stairs, Prince Eristan was delighted to find Cordelia, Lord Stephen, and Lord Keidric waiting for them. He grabbed his sister and hugged her.

"Are you all right?" he asked in a quiet voice. "Did they treat you well?"

"I was placed in a cell just as you were," she whispered. "It was scary and I didn't sleep well, but I suppose that I am all right."

"My friends, again I apologize for the rude treatment at our hands," the magistrate said tentatively, "and deeply regret that we have accommodated you in such a fashion. I will do my best to make you as comfortable as possible throughout the day and trust that we will speedily arrive at the truth of the matter when the High Council convenes." He smiled apologetically. "And now we must hurry, for I am sure that you are in need of refreshment."

Sir Reginald caught Prince Eristan's eye and gave him a wink as if to say, "This might turn out all right, after all."

After freshening up and enjoying a delicious breakfast in the great hall, Prince Eristan and his companions followed Lord Wallace to the throne room. Scowling and fretful, King Vladimir waited on the throne with his six bodyguards in attendance. Eight magistrates in dark robes sat at a long table, and a court scribe sat at a tiny desk, but otherwise, the vast chamber was empty. Six empty chairs stood across from the magistrates' table, and the Chief Magistrate indicated with a sweep of his hand that Prince Eristan and his company were to be seated.

He strode to the table and conferred with the other magistrates. Sir Reginald leaned close to Eristan. "All nine of the magistrates on the High Council were appointed by your father," he whispered. "Every one of them is a man of wisdom and virtue. They will do what is right for the kingdom."

Lord Wallace conferred with the other magistrates for another minute or two and then approached the throne. "Your Majesty, as Chief Magistrate of Cheswold I have called this special session of the High Council in order to more fully examine the claims of the said heir to the throne of Cheswold, the alleged Prince Eristan. Royal Cheswoldian law holds that if the youth can indeed establish his identity as Prince Eristan, son of the late King William of Cheswold, he is to take to throne upon the tenth of next month.

"May I be the first to express the appreciation of the High Council for your diligence in carrying out your duties as regent. You have taken the place of our beloved king and provided leadership for Cheswold, and for that we are grateful."

"If I may say so," Vladimir interrupted, when Lord Wallace paused for breath, "the lad is an imposter. Many years have passed since anyone has heard from Prince Eristan. There is no way this youth can establish his identity as the missing prince. This special session is a travesty."

"If it please Your Majesty, allow the High Council to examine the evidence before reaching a conclusion," Lord Wallace requested.

He turned to Prince Eristan. "If you please, step forward, my lord." Eristan did so, and the magistrate seated him in a chair directly in front of the magistrates' table. "Please state your name, my lord."

"Prince Eristan of Cheswold, son of the late King William of Cheswold."

"Prince Eristan of Cheswold, what proof of your identity do you have to submit to the High Council?"

Eristan took a deep breath. "I have no proof, sire."

"Then how do you expect to convince the High Council that you are indeed Prince Eristan, crown prince of Cheswold?"

Eristan was uncomfortable. "I do not know, sire. Up until last month I thought I was Dathan, son of Willis, a peasant carpenter."

The Chief magistrate looked confused. The magistrates at the table looked annoyed and whispered among themselves. "Sire, you talk in riddles," Lord Wallace declared. "Please explain the matter, or I shall dismiss this Council."

"If you please, sir," Eristan replied, "ask Sir Reginald to explain the matter and provide the evidence as to my identity."

Lord Wallace let out his breath in a long sigh and turned to Sir Reginald. "If you please, sire, take the stand." He glanced at Prince Eristan. "Sire, please excuse yourself so that this man may give his testimony."

When Sir Reginald took his seat, Lord Wallace said, "Please state your name for the Council, sire."

"I am Sir Reginald of Orwyn. For nine years I served the late King William as the castle constable in charge of the garrisons of knights defending Barrington Castle."

King Vladimir leaped to his feet. "If you are Reginald of Orwyn, sir, you shall be charged with treason to the crown, for you deserted your king on the night when he needed you most! You fled the castle, sir, rather than fight the king's enemies! Once your cowardice and guilt are established, Sir Reginald, you shall be hung as a traitor."

Reginald calmly shook his head. "I am no traitor, sire. My men and I fought valiantly for Barrington Castle that night, and I was prepared to give my life for my beloved king. When it became obvious that we would lose the castle that night, King William relieved me of my command and then commissioned me to take his two children, the young Prince Eristan and Princess Cordelia, to safety. Taking the two children, my wife and I fled the castle via a route that I am not at liberty to disclose. We took the twins to safety, and the next day we fled to a shire in northern Cheswold. I became a carpenter and raised the twins as my own children. My wife died the year after we—"

"The castle was surrounded, sir," Vladimir interrupted. "There was no way out of the castle. Your account does not ring true."

"There is a way," Sir Reginald insisted. "And though I cannot reveal that to the High Council, I can prove my story. I can also present evidence of Prince Eristan's identity."

"What evidence do you offer, sir?" the king asked scornfully.

Sir Reginald reached within his doublet and withdrew a gleaming object fashioned of solid gold. "The golden dagger belonging to the late King William himself," he replied quietly, holding the weapon aloft so that all could see it, "given to me the very night of the battle. It was given as a token of the trust the king was placing in me."

King Vladimir was scornful. "The dagger proves nothing. I am told that the rest of the crown jewels are in the hands of the Karnivans, yet possession of the jewels gives them no right to the throne." He eyed the dagger for a long moment. "Is this all you have to offer as proof?"

"If it please the king and the High Council, I would ask that His Majesty and all nine magistrates accompany me to the castle keep, whereupon I shall present the rest of my evidence. I would also ask that the royal twins and my three companions be allowed to attend us as witnesses."

"This is most irregular," King Vladimir complained.

Lord Wallace stepped to the table and conferred briefly with the other magistrates. "The High Council grants your request," he announced. He looked at the king. "With your permission, sire, we will move to the keep and we would ask that you accompany us."

Vladimir shrugged. "I suppose that we will have no peace around here until we lay this matter to rest."

The assembly left the throne room with the High Council leading the way. Prince Eristan and Princess Cordelia walked side by side, and Cordelia slipped her hand into her brother's arm. "The king is so frightful, isn't he?" she whispered. "He acts like he doesn't believe a word you say."

"He knows that he will have to give up the throne if I can prove my identity as the crown prince," Eristan whispered back. "Of course he's going to challenge our story."

"Do you think Pa actually has proof of your identity?" she asked, with eyes wide with worry.

"He must have something or he wouldn't have said it," Eristan returned, "although I can't imagine what it possibly could be."

After a walk of two or three minutes, the magistrates paused before a massive iron door. "Sir Reginald, we have complied with your request," the Chief Magistrate said in a loud voice. "Pray tell, sire, what proof do you offer?"

"Bear witness that I have not set foot inside Barrington Castle in nearly fourteen years," Reginald replied, "and that I have not had access to the keep during that time. What I am about to show you was placed within the keep by the late King William himself on the very night in which he was slain."

"How do we know that you have not bribed a guard?" King Vladimir demanded. "Your statement proves nothing."

"The penalty for such a deed is death, Your Majesty," one of the magistrates replied. "No amount of money would entice a man to do that. And one guard alone could not gain access to the keep, for he would need both keys."

Sir Reginald turned to Lord Wallace. "If you would, sire, open the keep."

The Chief Magistrate stepped to the iron door, produced a large key from within the folds of his robe, and inserted it into a keyhole. When he turned it, a loud click sounded in the corridor. He then turned to one of the guards on duty, who produced a second key. Taking the key from the guard, the magistrate unlocked the door and then returned the key.

The hinges creaked as the massive door swung slowly open. Lord Wallace stood to one side and handed a lamp to King Vladimir. "Your Majesty. . . ."

Bearing two lamps, the guards followed King Vladimir into the keep, followed by the nine magistrates, and then the rest of the company. Prince Eristan and Princess Cordelia crowded in eagerly to find themselves standing in a small, windowless room. Prince Eristan held his breath and stared about the room in awe. The flickering flame of the lamps illuminated glittering stores of treasure. A line of huge wooden chests against one wall held gleaming piles of golden coins; the opposite wall held shelf after shelf of smaller chests filled with sparkling diamonds, rubies, emeralds, sapphires and pearls. The far end of the treasure vault was piled high with large bars of gold and silver. Row after row of pigeonhole compartments on the wall above the cache of gold and silver ingots held scores of rolled parchments.

"Lord Wallace," Sir Reginald requested, "would you do us the honor of retrieving the document prepared by the late King William? Would you be so kind as to remove the center drawer from the counting desk before you?"

The magistrate slid the drawer out and then turned to Sir Reginald. "What next, sire?"

Sir Reginald took the drawer from his hands. "Sire, if you will reach to the back of the opening, you will find a small space between the top and the back of the desk. It's to the right side. You will feel the edge of a rolled parchment. Would you remove it, sire?"

Lord Wallace inserted his hand into the opening, felt around for a moment, and then gave an exclamation of surprise. "Aye, there is something here!"

"Would you remove it, sire?"

Moments later, the magistrate held up a rolled parchment.

"I will ask you to read it to us, sire, but first, let me ask you this. You have been Chief Magistrate of Cheswold for eighteen years. During that time, you have had ample opportunity to read many documents signed by the late King William. Would you, sire, be able to recognize William's handwriting, and in particular, his signature? Could you identify them, sire, with certainty?"

Lord Wallace paused and considered the question. "Aye, sir, I could."

"Would you then, sire, open the document and identify the signature and the royal seal as genuine?"

The magistrate unrolled the parchment and then exclaimed, "It's been torn in two! Half of the document is missing!"

Sir Reginald calmly reached inside his doublet and withdrew a small, brass cylinder. Opening it, he took out a tightly rolled parchment. "I have the other half," he told the assembly, "given to me by King William. He did this to help establish my identity."

Lord Wallace placed the two pieces side by side on the table and then carefully slid them together. "They fit perfectly," he announced. "They definitely belong together as halves of the same parchment."

The Chief Magistrate bent over the document and studied it for a long moment. "It's genuine," he declared at last. "This document is written in William's own hand, signed by him, and sealed with the royal signet."

"You're certain."

Lord Wallace glanced again at the parchment. "I am certain."

"What does it say?" a magistrate asked.

"Sire, if you would keep the document," Sir Reginald said to Lord Wallace, "I would suggest that we adjourn to the throne room. I'm sure we would all find it far more comfortable."

Prince Eristan's heart was in his throat as the company hurried back to the throne room. Princess Cordelia fell into step beside him. "What do you suppose is in the document?" she whispered. "How can Pa use it to prove that you are the crown prince?"

Her brother shook his head. "I have no idea, but I suppose we'll know in a moment."

Chapter Four

King Vladimir's face was a mask of fury as he followed the magistrates back to the throne room of Barrington Castle, but Eristan also saw the haunting fear in his eyes. Clearly, the regent was worried.

Upon reaching the throne room, King Vladimir once again took his place upon the throne while the rest of the company took their original seats. Lord Wallace stood before the throne and unrolled the parchment. "With your permission, sire, I shall read the document." King Vladimir waved his hand in a careless gesture.

Lord Wallace cleared his throat and began to read from the parchment.

"The battle rages for Barrington Castle and my time is measured, so I must write this as hastily as possible. Tonight I place my jeweled dagger into the hands of my constable, Sir Reginald of Orwyn, as a token of the confidence that I have in him. I am entrusting the safety of my two children, Prince Eristan and Princess Cordelia, into Sir Reginald's hands with instructions to flee the castle and secure my children. In the event of my death, in accordance with royal law, Lord Vladimir of Stocklin is to become my regent and ascend the throne.

"Upon his sixteenth birthday—" Lord Wallace looked up from the document at this point. "The date is smudged, but it is a matter of royal record." He lowered his eyes to the parchment and continued reading.

". . . my son, Prince Eristan, is to ascend the throne as king of Cheswold. Prince Eristan's identity may be established and verified in the following way: he has a large, triangular birthmark behind his right knee and a boat-shaped birthmark beneath his left shoulder blade. Before Eristan takes the throne, the court physician shall examine him and make a determination regarding the genuineness of his birthmarks.

"In the event that Eristan is deceased or cannot be located by his sixteenth birthday, Lord Vladimir shall retain the throne until his own death or until such a time as he is incapable of governing.

"Given by my hand, signed by the same, and affixed with my royal seal, this document is irrevocable and shall stand as Cheswoldian law. By decree of His Majesty, King William of Cheswold."

Silence reigned in the throne room as the Chief Magistrate finished reading the document. All eyes darted to King Vladimir as Lord Wallace re-rolled the parchment.

Vladimir cleared his throat. "The document shall be examined as to its genuineness," he declared. "Methinks that it is spurious."

Lord Wallace nodded. "As you wish, sire. The magistrates are already assembled."

"It shall be examined by magistrates of my own choosing."

The Chief Magistrate shook his head. "This falls under the jurisdiction of the High Council, sire. Under Cheswoldian law, sire, only the High Council shall make rulings regarding the disposition of the throne." He stepped to the table and spread the parchment before the other magistrates. "Your decision, gentlemen. Is this document genuine? Does it indeed bear the signature and royal seal of the late King William?"

The eight men stood to their feet, surrounded the table, and bent their heads close to the parchment as they examined it. The only sound in the chamber was a low murmur of voices as they discussed it. After several long, tense moments, Lord Wallace approached the throne with the parchment in his hand.

"Our decision is unanimous, my lord. The document is genuine."

Vladimir's face stiffened and he took on the appearance of an angry lion. "The lad's identity has not been established."

Lord Wallace turned to one of the guards. "Summon the royal physician."

"Aye, sire." The guard hurried from the room.

Sterling leaned over to Prince Eristan. "Do you have those two birthmarks?"

Prince Eristan shrugged. "How should I know? I've never seen my own back and I've never examined the back of my knee."

Moments later the royal physician hurried into the throne room with a small leather satchel. He looked around the throne room. "What is the emergency?"

Lord Wallace held up one hand. "You were not summoned to attend to a medical emergency, sir, but we do have a matter of great importance." He gestured toward Prince Eristan. "If you please, sir, examine the back of this lad's right knee."

The physician was perplexed. "His knee, sire?"

The magistrate smiled. "Aye, sir, his knee."

The physician glanced up at King Vladimir and then at Prince Eristan. "If you please, I shall take the lad to my chambers—"

"We can do it here," Prince Eristan interrupted. "Exposing my knee will not be an issue of modesty." He reached down with both hands, seized the fabric of his leggings, and ripped the garment open behind the right knee. He then stood to his feet. "There. I'm ready."

The physician knelt behind Prince Eristan. "What am I looking for, sire?"

"Just tell us what you see," Lord Wallace instructed.

The man opened the rip in the fabric and touched Eristan's leg. "The lad has a large, triangular birthmark, but other than that, I see nothing unusual. What am I looking for?"

"Is the birthmark real?" King Vladimir asked sharply.

"Real, Your Majesty? Why would it not be real?"

"Perhaps it was painted on by some devious individual," Vladimir suggested. "Perhaps it is just a stain of some sort."

The physician was puzzled, but he opened his satchel and removed a white cloth and a small vial. Placing a few drops of liquid on the cloth, he rubbed the birthmark vigorously, and then examined the cloth. "It's real, sire, though I don't understand what this is all about."

"Examine his back," Lord Wallace requested.

Prince Eristan was already pulling his doublet up in back. "Look beneath my left shoulder blade," he told the man.

"I find here another birthmark," the physician said a moment later, "shaped rather like a . . . a boat, I would say."

"Is it real?" King Vladimir demanded.

The physician gave him a strange look and then proceeded to rub the skin vigorously with the cloth. "It's real, Your Majesty. What is this all about, my lord?"

"Thank you for your assistance, sir," Lord Wallace told him. "You may be excused." Picking up his satchel, the physician shook his head in bewilderment as he left the room.

Lord Wallace stepped to the magistrates' table and conferred with the other men for several minutes. Tension filled the chamber. At last, he advanced toward the throne. "Your Majesty, in the opinion of the High Council, the lad's identity has been duly established. He is indeed Prince Eristan of Cheswold, son of the late King William of Cheswold, crown prince and heir to the throne. Royal Cheswoldian law requires that you surrender the throne upon the dawn of Prince Eristan's sixteenth birthday, the tenth of next month."

"Just like that, aye?" King Vladimir said bitterly. "I've been your king for fourteen years, and just like that you're going to attempt to depose me?"

"We are following the dictates of the late King William, sire. You took the throne with the understanding that you were a regent and would rule Cheswold until Prince Eristan's sixteenth birthday. The High Council is simply following royal Cheswoldian law in rendering this decision, sire. You have no choice but to step down upon the tenth of next month, sire."

"I do have one other option," King Vladimir growled. He gestured toward one of the guards. "Admit our guests."

As the court watched in silence, the guard hurried to the far end of the throne room and flung open the double doors. Two officers in full dress uniform stepped into the throne room.

"I defy the High Council's decision," King Vladimir snarled, "and I have no intention of surrendering the throne of Cheswold. You know Captain Alexander and Captain Randor. They have assured me that the armies of Cheswold will stand with me. Lord Wallace, the might of Cheswold is behind me and you will not force me from the throne."

Lord Wallace was aghast. "S-Sire, you would defy Cheswoldian law? You would bring civil war to Cheswold in your attempt to keep the throne?"

"Aye, if it comes to that!" Vladimir roared. Leaping to his feet, he turned to his guards. "I want the High Council arrested and thrown into the dungeon, as well as this impertinent young prince and all his entourage. The throne of Cheswold is mine, and I have no intention of stepping down!"

Chapter Five

Prince Eristan's heart pounded furiously as the guards drew their swords and moved forward to arrest him and his companions a second time. *Vladimir has no intention of surrendering the throne,* he thought in dismay.

"Wait!" Lord Wallace cried, and the guards hesitated. Lord Wallace glared at King Vladimir. "Before you attempt to have us arrested, sire, may I remind you that what you are about to do is in defiance of royal law! The late King William decreed in writing that the throne of Cheswold is to be surrendered to Prince Eristan upon his sixteenth birthday. If you defy that edict, sire, you defy royal Cheswoldian law!"

The regent shrugged. "Perhaps I no longer care to abide under royal Cheswoldian law, sir," he replied scornfully. "I am still the king and I will do as I please. The power of the military is behind me."

"Then I shall be forced to call another power into play," the Chief Magistrate replied sternly. He raised one hand and gestured, and a door opened on the far side of the throne room. Three more Cheswoldian captains strode into the room. "Sire, I suspected that you might take this stance, and so I prepared in advance. You know Captains Vance, Trevarr, and Orwyn.

All three have already assured me that their battalions will fully support King Eristan, once he is sworn into office. Three battalions against two, sire. Sixty percent of the army sides with the new king."

"We are not afraid of battle, sir, if it comes to that," King Vladimir asserted scornfully. "We are ready. I tell you again, I will not concede the throne."

"Would you bring war to Cheswold, sire? Civil war would damage and weaken the kingdom, sire, at the very time when we must be united and strong. Grimlor and the Karnivans are preparing to invade, and we must be prepared."

"The Chief Magistrate is right, sire." The comment came from Captain Orwyn. "Civil war would devastate the nation. Would you attempt to hold the throne, sire, even if meant the destruction of Cheswold?"

King Vladimir was silent.

Lord Wallace stepped closer to the throne. "May I remind you, sire, that if you acquiesce and surrender the throne peacefully, your name will remain in the history records as one of the benefactors of our great nation. A stipend of five thousand klorins will be provided annually from the royal treasury, and a regal mansion will be built for you. The provisions for such are already written into royal law.

"Should you refuse, sire, and bring civil war to Cheswold, you do irreparable damage to this kingdom. Your name will have a blot upon it throughout history. And I promise you this—the High Council will make certain that your stipend is taken away and that all plans for a mansion are rescinded. Think it through, sire. Should you defy royal law, the costs will be enormous—both to you and to this kingdom."

King Vladimir eyed the three captains as if considering an attempt to sway them to his side. The throne room was silent as everyone present waited breathlessly for the regent's decision. Tension filled the chamber. Prince Eristan's heart pounded with anticipation as he awaited the regent's response.

At last, King Vladimir spoke. "I will hold this throne," he announced, "until the tenth of next month. At that time I will peacefully surrender the throne to Prince Eristan."

Audible sighs of relief were heard across the throne room.

Prince Eristan approached the throne. "Thank you, sire. I believe that your decision was made in the best interests of Cheswold and will benefit the kingdom. Will you assist me in the transition? You have fourteen years of experience, sire—will you allow me the benefit of that experience?"

King Vladimir sighed heavily. "I will do my best, my prince."

"I am greatly relieved," Prince Eristan said to Sir Reginald, as he and the company followed King Vladimir's steward to the special chambers prepared for them. "Had Vladimir continued to resist, this would have turned into civil war. Cheswold would not have survived that."

Sir Reginald nodded. "Emmanuel be praised that it did not go that far."

"Why did he suddenly change his mind?" Cordelia asked.

Lord Stephen chuckled. "Three battalions against two, my lady. Vladimir knew that he was hopelessly outnumbered."

Reginald smiled. "There was also the matter of the annual stipend and the mansion. He wasn't about to risk losing those."

"Well, no matter what the reason," Prince Eristan replied, "hopefully the matter is behind us and the plans for my coronation can go forward. I want the transition to go as quickly and smoothly as possible. In fact, I would hope that we could accomplish it without the Karnivans getting wind of it."

"Sire, I would proceed immediately with the plans for the border security," Lord Keidric said. "And it would be best to review the troops as soon as possible. We need to know in just what state of readiness we find the army."

"I agree," Prince Eristan replied.

"With your permission, sire, I will arrange it with the captains," Lord Keidric continued. "I'll ask them for the earliest possible date at which a review can take place."

"Excellent, sir," the young prince replied. "I would also ask that each of you regularly send petitions to King Emmanuel, asking him for wisdom and for protection for Cheswold as we make this transition."

The twins and Sterling sat at King Vladimir's table in the palace that night, directly across from Sir Reginald, Lord Keidric, and Lord Stephen. King Vladimir sat at the head of the table, to the twins' left, while the five captains sat to their right. Nearly a score of lords and ladies filled out the list.

Smiling servants moved among the tables, serving roast pheasant and duck, fillets of fresh water fish, garden vegetables and roasted yams, and a vast variety of breads, fritters, muffins, and other baked delights. Princess Cordelia leaned over to her brother and whispered, "Did you ever see such a fancy table? Even Windstone Castle wasn't like this! The table service is solid gold. And look at the crystal."

"Look at the food," Eristan replied. "That's what matters. This is a feast fit for a king!"

"You *are* a king, silly," she replied with a quiet giggle. "Or at least you soon will be."

"So, my prince," King Vladimir said in a loud voice, "are you making plans for your coronation ceremonies? This is your big moment, you know."

"I'd like to keep the ceremonies to a minimum," Eristan replied. "We'll plan for the coronation to be as simple as possible. My primary focus will be on securing the borders and making sure that the armies are prepared against an invasion by the Karnivans. If we were to host extravagant ceremonies, the royal treasury would be depleted in no time, leaving no monies for military needs."

"Well put, sire," one captain remarked.

"Oh, I disagree, sire," a thin voice said, and Eristan turned to the speaker, a young man seated across the table and one place to the right. "Allow me to introduce myself, my lord," the young man said. "I am Lord Aric, prime minister of Cheswold. It is an honor to serve you, sire."

"You're—you're the prime minister?" Eristan echoed. "How old are you, Lord Aric?"

"I am twenty-one years of age," Aric replied.

The young prince was surprised. "That is quite an office for one so young."

"Why do you find that unusual, sire? You are not yet sixteen, yet I am told that you are to be our king."

Prince Eristan grinned sheepishly. "I see your point." He laughed. "I will say no more about your age."

"Lord Aric has been an outstanding prime minister," King Vladimir boomed, "and he wins favor with the younger members of the kingdom; thus they support our policies."

Lord Aric laughed. "My father was the castle steward under your father. When I was little I used to sit upon your father's lap and help him make decisions. Or at least, I thought I was helping him." He laughed again. "I do know that one time I chose the color for the new draperies in the throne room and King William actually ordered the color that I chose."

Prince Eristan smiled as he looked back at Lord Aric. "You said that you disagree with my intentions to keep the ceremonies simple and economical."

"Aye, my lord. Your coronation is your one big moment—make the most of it. The people of Cheswold love pomp and ceremony, they love pageantry, and they love celebrations and feasts. I would suggest that you make this event as big and elaborate as possible. Plan parades and festivals and extravagant feasts. Take the throne amid the most colorful pageantry they have ever seen them. There should be music and feasting and dancing in the streets. Indulge these people a little and they will love you forever."

"How would we pay for all this?" Prince Eristan asked. "As I mentioned, such pageantry would drain the royal treasury."

"Simply raise their taxes," the youthful prime minister replied casually. "Just don't let them realize that they are the ones paying for the festivities."

"The fond memories of an extravagant feast are soon forgotten when the bitterness of high taxes sets in," Sir Reginald responded.

Lord Aric smirked. "You'll find that for the most part, the populace of Cheswold have very short memories; thus, a leader can get away with almost anything." He turned to Prince Eristan. "Again, my lord, may I suggest that you make the most of this opportunity. Plan the biggest, most extravagant coronation you can possibly imagine. Feasting and dancing and parades and pageantry will win their hearts faster than anything."

King Vladimir raised his crystal goblet. "A toast to the new king. May your reign be long and glorious."

Later that evening, Lord Keidric slipped up beside Prince Eristan as they walked back to the royal apartments. "May I offer you a bit of advice, my lord?"

"Aye, certainly," Eristan replied. "What is it?"

"Sire, I would advise that you refrain from sharing any of your plans with King Vladimir. For instance, you mentioned your plans to secure the borders and make certain that the armies are in readiness for an invasion by Grimlor and the Karnivans. If I may be so bold as to suggest it, sire, I would not share such information with him. We don't know that we can trust him."

"I don't trust him," Cordelia chimed in. "He has shifty eyes. Every time he looks at you, he looks away quickly."

"He is the king of Cheswold," Prince Eristan argued. "Are you saying that he cannot be trusted with national secrets?"

"There are those who suspect that he is in league with Grimlor," the nobleman said quietly, "and that perhaps he is secretly aiding the Karnivans in their attempt to take over Cheswold and merge the two kingdoms."

"Are you saying that he is a traitor? Why would my father have chosen such a man as regent?"

"That was fourteen years ago," Sir Reginald commented. "A man can change dramatically in fourteen years. I knew Vladimir before I took you and your sister into hiding, and he is not the same man. Someone or something has changed him."

Two days later, Prince Eristan and Sterling sat in the reviewing stands with Sir Reginald, Lord Keidric, and Lord

Stephen as the five battalions of the royal Cheswoldian army paraded past. The five commanding captains sat in a row directly behind them. As the second battalion marched past, Sir Reginald leaned close to Prince Eristan. "It's worse than I imagined," he said in a quiet voice. "Their uniforms are mismatched and look as if they were issued forty years ago, and their weapons are in worse condition than the uniforms. Half of the men are out of step. And notice their faces. These men look as if they know that their units are in bad shape and yet don't care. This is the most poorly trained, poorly equipped army I have ever seen!"

One of the captains leaned forward. "King Vladimir has refused to provide the funding we need for uniforms and arms," he growled. "His Majesty has ordered us to curtail our training exercises to the point that these men are totally unprepared for battle. It's as if King Vladimir has deliberately weakened our forces."

"Hold your tongue, sir," another captain told him.

"You and I both know that it's true," the first replied. "The army of Cheswold must be the poorest trained, poorest equipped army in the history of Terrestria!" He turned back to Prince Eristan. "And now you know, sire, why King Vladimir refused to attend this review with us."

Prince Eristan let out his breath in a long sigh as the battalions continued to parade past. Fear mounted within him as he realized just how ill-prepared Cheswold would be to repel an invasion by Lord Grimlor and the Karnivans. How could King Vladimir have allowed the army to reach such a state? At last, he spoke. "I want to see their battle skills. Have some of the men conduct a skirmish for us."

Fifteen minutes later, all five battalions stood at attention on the parade grounds as Prince Eristan and his companions passed among them. "You, sir," the young prince said to a lieutenant, "have your unit step forward and then I will select five men to demonstrate their skills in swordsmanship."

"Aye, sire," the officer replied, and barked an order. Eristan watched in dismay as the men shuffled forward. He walked along the ragged line, selecting five men at random. "You five will represent your unit."

He then selected another unit and chose five men from among them. "Pair off with a man from the other unit," he ordered. "I want you to skirmish so that I may see your swordsmanship."

The soldiers paired off. Eristan shook his head as one soldier borrowed a sword from his neighbor in order to participate. The selected men began to fight and it quickly became obvious that their swordsmanship was greatly lacking. Slow and clumsy, the men swung their swords with the same carelessness with which they had marched. Eristan watched with a growing sense of dismay.

"Pathetic," the young prince said at last. "Some of these men act as if they have never before handled a sword."

"We will begin extensive training at once, sire," Captain Vance asserted. "We will train night and day until you are satisfied that the troops are battle ready."

Prince Eristan scanned the five captains. "How are *your* battle skills, gentlemen? You are officers, but how sharp is your swordsmanship?"

He motioned to Captain Vance. "Please allow me to use your sword." The man complied and handed the weapon to Prince Eristan.

Eristan nodded toward Captain Trevarr. "Draw your sword, sir."

The man looked stunned. "My lord?"

"Draw your sword," the young prince repeated. "I want you to go against me in a skirmish."

"Sire?"

"Draw your sword, sir," Eristan said sharply. "Prepare to defend yourself. You and I will skirmish for the benefit of the men."

Drawing his sword, the captain abruptly leaped toward Eristan, swinging the weapon in a broad horizontal cut. The young prince easily parried the attack, knocking the captain slightly off balance. "I will not humiliate you in front of your men, sir," Prince Eristan said in a low voice, "but I could have ended the skirmish right there had I chosen to follow through. Give me your best, Captain."

The two continued to skirmish and Prince Eristan quickly saw that the captain's skills were not up to standards. The man's movements were stiff and precise, as if he had not practiced in years, and the young prince predicted every move before he made it. Finally, Prince Eristan advanced on the captain, driving him backward with a fast series of slices and combinations, though he withheld some of his speed to keep from completely overpowering the man. Sweating and gasping for breath, the captain struggled to defend himself. At last, Prince Eristan called a halt to the exercise. "Thank you, Captain. That will be all."

Panting like a winded horse, Captain Trevarr nodded and sheathed his sword, obviously embarrassed by his own lack of skill.

"Dismiss your battalions," the young prince ordered the captains, "and then we shall talk."

Ten minutes later, Prince Eristan sat in the reviewing stand as the five officers stood nervously before him. "Gentlemen," he said, "It's worse than I had imagined. Our armies are not ready for battle. Should the Karnivans invade Cheswold today, they would find us totally unprepared, for our swordsmanship is shoddy and our battle skills are greatly lacking. And if the *captains* are not current with their skills, how can we expect the troops to be trained and ready?"

The five captains waited in tense silence.

"We will have to begin training immediately," the young prince said to Sir Reginald, "though I have no idea how we will go about it. If the officers themselves are not properly trained, who will train the troops?"

Sterling stepped close to Prince Eristan. "I think your question was just answered," he said with a look of astonished delight upon his face. "Look who's coming!"

Prince Eristan looked up to see a small cart slowly making its way up the steep approach to the main gate of the castle. Pulled by a small donkey, the cart carried an old man and woman. The young prince stared in disbelief. His heart began to pound. The occupants of the cart were too far away for him to recognize, but he knew at a glance who they were.

"Miriam and Melzar!" he exclaimed in astonishment. "Melzar is alive!"

Chapter Six

Tears of joy flowed down Princess Cordelia's face as she embraced Melzar and Miriam again and again. "It's so wonderful to have you here!" she exclaimed for the third time. "It's so good to see you again! I can't believe that you're really here!"

"Sire," Prince Eristan said to Melzar, "we thought you were dead! When the Karnivan knight shot you with the crossbow, all three of us thought that you had been killed. Sire, we never would have left you in the field if we had had any idea that you were still alive."

The old man grinned broadly. "I suppose I would have died that night, save for my dear Miriam. When she returned from the birth of the baby she couldn't find me in the house, so she went looking for me. Somehow she dragged me back to the house and nursed me back to health."

Miriam hugged Prince Eristan and Sterling. "It's so good to see you again." She looked on Eristan with wondering eyes. "Dathan, we hear that you are to be the king of Cheswold. Is that true, dear?"

Prince Eristan laughed and nodded. "Unbelievable, isn't it? Imagine me as the king! But it's true. My real name is Prince Eristan and my father was King William. Cordelia and I are the long-lost twins of Cheswold."

"You know how news travels," Melzar said. "We heard that the long-lost prince and princess had been found and so we came immediately."

Prince Eristan stared at him. "Are you saying . . . are you saying that you knew that it was us?"

The old man nodded.

"Did you know when we stayed with you? Did you know that I was the crown prince?"

"Aye. Why do you think I spent so much time training you in the use of the sword?"

Prince Eristan shook his head in wonder. "Why didn't you tell me? Cordelia and I had no idea."

"You wouldn't have been ready for that information," Melzar replied quietly.

"Pa, this is Melzar and Miriam," Prince Eristan said, as Sir Reginald walked up just then. "We stayed with them when Sterling was hurt. Melzar trained me in the use of the sword."

"Melzar and Miriam, this is Sir Reginald, though Cordelia and I call him Pa. He's the one who took us from Barrington Castle on the night when our father was killed, and he raised us as his own children. He used to be the castle constable, and will be once again when I take the throne."

Sir Reginald exchanged polite greetings with the elderly couple. "It is so good to see you again," he told them. "It has been so long. I deeply appreciate what you did for Cordelia and Eristan."

"Pa, Melzar is a master swordsman," Eristan said excitedly. "He could train the troops."

"Would you, sir?" Sir Reginald asked.

"I would be delighted," Melzar replied. "With His Majesty's permission, of course."

"You would not only have my permission," Prince Eristan said delightedly, "you would have my undying gratitude. The troops desperately need training, and no one is more qualified than you for the task. You and Miriam would have a solar in the castle, of course."

"And Ebenezer would have a stall in the royal stables?" the old man asked, with a mischievous twinkle in his eye.

"Of course. Your donkey is as welcome as you, for he brought you here."

"I thank you," Melzar replied. He was thoughtful for a long moment. "We can start with thirty officers," he said, "six from each battalion. We will train for five hours each morning. They can then train the troops each afternoon. I will train cavalry units in the afternoons.

"Once the thirty officers are properly trained, I will repeat the process with thirty more. The training will be intensive and quite demanding, for we have no time to lose." He looked at Prince Eristan. "When can we start?"

"The morning after my coronation," the young prince replied immediately. "We will waste no time. As you said, we cannot afford to wait."

Melzar nodded. "As you wish, my lord." He gazed in wonder around the castle courtyard, taking in the verdant, well-manicured lawns and exquisite flower gardens, the elegant fountains and statuary, and the gleaming marble walkways leading to the well-kept orchards. "What a magnificent castle, lad. This place is incredible."

Prince Eristan laughed. "It is magnificent, to be sure. Barrington Castle is the finest in Terrestria!"

The old man eyed the elegant palace in the distance. "Is the palace as magnificent as it looks from here?"

"Aye, that it is." Prince Eristan laughed again. "I think I'm going to enjoy being the king of Cheswold!"

Melzar gave him a strange look. "Why do you take the throne, lad?"

Prince Eristan stared at him. "I don't understand your question, sir."

"For what reason do you seek to be king?"

"I am the son of King William, rightful king of Cheswold. As his son, I am the heir to the throne."

"Aye, I understand that, lad, but that's not what I'm asking. What is your purpose as king?"

"Sir?"

"Do you plan to take the throne to accommodate yourself and live a life of wealth and luxury, or do you plan to serve your people? Do you plan to make a name for yourself, or will you strengthen the kingdom? You have not come to the kingdom to serve yourself, Prince Eristan. In a way, you are simply the steward of King Emmanuel, chosen to rule Cheswold that you might serve him by serving his people. You must decide if you will serve yourself or serve your people."

The young prince was silent.

"Oh, Eristan," the old man continued, "determine at the outset that you will serve your people. As the king of Cheswold you will live a life of wealth and privilege. Enjoy it, for there is nothing wrong with that, but never forget that you were commissioned to be a servant, not a great monarch."

Sir Reginald approached at that moment. "Excuse me, my lord, but you and I have a meeting with the captains in just a few minutes."

Prince Eristan nodded. "Thank you, Pa." He turned to Melzar. "I would like for you to attend this briefing, sire. I want to introduce you to the captains of my army."

Melzar smiled. "Whose army?"

The young prince laughed. "All right, the captains of the army of Cheswold!"

Together the three walked to the large council chamber behind the great hall. They entered to find four of the captains waiting for them, along with Lord Aric, the young prime minister, and other dignitaries. The assembly stood to their feet as the young prince entered, and remained standing until he had taken a seat at the table beside Sir Reginald.

Captain Randor walked in at that moment with a tall, broad-chested officer. "Your Highness," Captain Randor said, "allow me to introduce Sir Winston, the castle constable. He and his garrisons have done a splendid job of protecting the castle. Sir Winston, Prince Eristan, crown prince of Cheswold and soon to be our king."

Sir Winston bowed slightly. "My lord."

"Winston is a personal favorite of Vladimir's," Sir Reginald said in a low voice, as he leaned close to Prince Eristan. "I'm told that they're both into falconry and do quite a bit of hunting together."

Captain Randor and Sir Winston took seats at the table.

"Sir Winston," Prince Eristan said, "how long have you been the castle constable?"

"Nearly twelve years, my lord."

"Sir Winston, I appreciate your years of service to the crown," the young prince continued, "and I do want you to know that I am grateful. However, Sir Reginald will serve as constable to the castle once I am on the throne."

The constable leaped to his feet with a look of agitation on his face. "Nay, my lord! Surely you can't mean this!"

"I'm sorry to break the news to you in this fashion," Eristan said calmly, "but that is the plan. Sir Reginald is to become constable."

"But, my lord, I have been the constable for nearly twelve years! The castle defenses are strong, sire, thanks to me. You—you can't do this, sire!"

"I can and I will. You are to be commended for your years of service, sir, but the position is being given to another. If you are a capable man and prove to be loyal to the crown, I'm sure that I can find another position for you."

Sir Winston's face tightened with anger. "Sire, this is prepos—" The big man stopped in mid-sentence and dropped to his seat without saying another word, but his face was red and his chest rose and fell rapidly. Prince Eristan knew that he was seething with rage.

"Well, Captains," the young prince said brightly in an attempt to dismiss the tension he felt, "the training in swordsmanship will proceed as we discussed. I want each of you to select the five most capable men from your battalion. On the morning following my coronation, I want you to report with your five men to the parade grounds for battle skills training. Melzar is a master swordsman, and he has agreed to train you.

"I have observed that many of our troops are not properly equipped and uniformed. We will also provide new uniforms and equipment to those units that need them the most."

He looked at Sir Winston. "I also want three men from both of your garrisons to attend the training. They will then train the rest of your men." The constable nodded stiffly.

"I have also asked Lord Keidric and Lord Stephen to stay here at the castle for the next two months to serve as my chief advisors as I take the throne and learn the affairs of the kingdom. They have both assured me that they will. King Vladimir has also promised me that I will have his help, so I am certain that the transition will be a smooth one."

He gestured toward Lord Aric. "How are the plans for Coronation Day coming?"

"Sire, the people of Cheswold are about to witness the grandest, the most glorious, the most magnificent coronation in the history of the kingdom! It will exceed your wildest expectations, sire. Three days of feasting, music, and dancing at Barrington Castle, with festivals and banquets in the major cities. There will be parades and pageantry that the populace will remember for a lifetime. This is a once in a lifetime event, sire, and we plan to make the most of it."

Prince Eristan glanced at Sir Reginald and then looked back to Lord Aric. "My instructions were to keep it simple, sir."

The young prime minister grinned as if immensely pleased with himself. "My objective, sire, is to overwhelm the populace with your magnificence and splendor, your wisdom and brilliance, your power and might. I want them to see for themselves just how wonderful life in Cheswold will be once we are under your reign and how fortunate they will be to have you as their king.

"You will have a long and prosperous reign, my lord. This is the only coronation that most of your people will ever witness. Let's make it a grand and glorious one that they will not soon forget."

Prince Eristan felt a swell of pride as he heard the prime minister's words. In the pride of the moment, he failed to realize that Lord Aric was using flattery to accomplish his own ends. He nodded. "We're eager to see for ourselves just what you have planned," he replied pleasantly, forgetting that Lord Aric had ignored his directive to keep the coronation simple.

Prince Eristan and the captains spent the next hour making plans for the transition of power as the young prince prepared to take the throne of Cheswold. After discussing the affairs of the kingdom with the men, asking their advice on different issues and fielding questions from them, the young prince dismissed the meeting. He walked out of the chamber to find Sterling waiting for him.

"Come with me to my solar so we can talk," Prince Eristan told him. "I've been so busy of late that we have hardly seen each other." He shook his head as if overwhelmed. "I'm starting to realize that being the king will not be as easy as it first seemed."

Sterling laughed. "But you're not about to give up your claim to the throne, I would wager?"

Prince Eristan laughed with him. "Not quite yet. I do want to try it for a week or two at least."

Prince Eristan and Sterling had reached the apartments which the young prince was occupying until King Vladimir would vacate the royal palace and renovations could be accomplished. "Come in and see this place," Prince Eristan invited his friend. "You won't believe your eyes."

After a quick tour that dazzled Sterling, Prince Eristan opened a drawer on an elaborate mahogany chiffonnier. "You remember this, I presume?" He lifted an item from the drawer and handed it to Sterling.

"The golden dagger of Cheswold," Sterling said reverently, cradling the relic in his hands. "But why do you have it here, rather than in the castle keep? Would it not be safer there?"

Prince Eristan shrugged. "No one knows that it is here, so I figure that it is safe enough. I enjoy looking at it from time to time—it reminds me of our journey across Cheswold and Karniva when the Karnivans were pursuing us." He chuckled. "I still remember the night you showed it to us. Cordelia and I were astounded to learn that you were carrying part of the crown jewels of Cheswold."

Sterling caressed the dagger. "Just imagine how astounded I was to learn that you and your sister were the long-lost royal twins, the princess and crown prince of Cheswold! I still cannot picture you as the king of Cheswold." He handed the gleaming dagger back to Prince Eristan. "Here. I am glad that this is no longer my responsibility."

The young prince carefully placed the golden dagger back in the chiffonnier. "I have to hurry to a meeting with the prime minister. He wants to go over the plans for my coronation."

"I almost forgot," Sterling said, pulling a small parchment from within his doublet. "A peasant gave me this for you."

Prince Eristan reached for the parchment. "A peasant?"

"Aye," Sterling replied, handing him the document. "He just walked up to me, bold as you please, and said, 'Give this to the new king, if you would, sire.' He then thrust the parchment into my hands and hurried away before I could ask him any questions."

"That's odd," the young prince replied. "And you have no idea who he was?"

"None."

Prince Eristan unrolled the parchment and spread it on top of the chiffonier. Both youth bent over it for a closer look. The document looked old and faded, but a cryptic message had been written in a bold, flowing script:

"In the city forbidden,
Doth the lion crouch deep.
A treasure lies hidden
Though far from the keep."

Prince Eristan stared at Sterling. "What does this mean? Is this some sort of prophecy?"

Sterling shook his head. "I have no idea." Placing his finger on the wrinkled parchment, he traced the words of the first line. "In the city forbidden . . . where would that be?"

"And what is the lion that crouches deep?"

Sterling shook his head a second time. "It's quite the cryptic message. Why would it say that the lion crouches *deep*? That's a strange choice of words. You might say that a lion crouches *low*, but you wouldn't say that it crouches *deep*."

Prince Eristan turned the parchment over. "Look at this symbol on the back. What do you think it is?"

"It looks like some sort of a star," Sterling began, and then promptly changed his mind. "Nay, it's a roundabout from a compass." A look of bewilderment crossed his face. "But why would you draw a compass roundabout on the back of a message such as this? This isn't a map."

"Perhaps it is," Eristan replied.

"How could this be a map?" Sterling scoffed. "There's no diagram of any kind, just a mysterious message about a lion and a hidden treasure. Where's the map in that?"

"Perhaps there's more to this than we are seeing," the young prince said, with a knowing smile, as though he knew something that his friend did not, though in reality he was just as baffled as Sterling. "Look—I have to hurry to that meeting with Lord Aric, but let's go over this again tonight after dinner. Are you interested?"

"I wouldn't miss it," Sterling replied, and his eyes reflected his enthusiasm.

"I'm going to hide the parchment in the drawer with the golden dagger," Prince Eristan told Sterling, "until we can study it tonight."

Once the two items were safely tucked away in the chiffonier drawer, Prince Eristan and Sterling hurried from the room. Prince Eristan opened the door to find Sir Winston standing at the door with his hand raised as if to knock. "Pardon me, sire," he said to Eristan, bowing low. "Would you spare just a moment of your valuable time? I have a matter that I must discuss with you."

"Is it urgent?" the young prince asked.

Sir Winston hesitated and then shrugged. "Nay, sire, not really. It's not a matter of life and death."

"I am late for an engagement with Lord Aric," Prince Eristan replied. "I value the opportunity to speak with you, sir, but what if we were to do it tomorrow morning, perhaps first thing after breakfast?"

"As you wish, sire." With a quick, stiff bow, Sir Winston turned and hurried away.

Prince Eristan looked at Sterling. "Not a word about the parchment to anyone, not even Cordelia."

Sterling nodded to show that he understood and was in full agreement. "Of course not."

Prince Eristan gave him a stern look. "Of course not . . . what?"

"What?"

Eristan maintained the look, though it was hard to keep from laughing. "Of course not, Your Majesty. Better get used to saying it, my friend."

Sterling stared at Eristan. "Are you . . . serious?"

"If you remember, I am going to be the king. I can have your head taken off at the slightest provocation." At that moment, he lost the battle and couldn't keep from laughing. "I'll see you at dinner, Sterling."

Chuckling to himself, the young prince hurried down the corridor toward his appointment with the prime minister.

At dinner that night Prince Eristan leaned over to Sterling, who was seated beside him at the dinner table. "Dinner is over, save for the sweets and confections. Are you going to stay? I'm anxious to have another look at . . . you know what."

Sterling scooted his chair back. "I'm ready when you are."

Sensing that something was afoot, Princess Cordelia leaned across the table and asked in a whisper, "What are you two up to?"

Prince Eristan shrugged casually. "Nothing. We're just going up to my solar to look at some old documents."

"You're up to something, Eristan," the girl insisted. "I can see it in your eyes. Now come on, out with it. Twins don't keep secrets from each other."

Eristan and Sterling looked at each other and then back to Cordelia. "All right, come along," the young prince told his sister. "Twins don't keep secrets."

The young princess followed Eristan and Sterling back to Eristan's solar. Moments later, Eristan carefully lifted the mysterious parchment from its hiding place, carried it to his desk, and spread it out. Cordelia stared. "What is it?"

"Some peasant gave it to Sterling this evening," Eristan told her. "We have no idea where it came from or what it means."

"In the city forbidden," the young princess read aloud, "doth the lion crouch deep. A treasure lies hidden, though far from the keep." She frowned and looked from Eristan to Sterling and then back to the parchment. "What in Terrestria? Who wrote it and what does it mean?"

"I just told you," her brother said impatiently. "We have no idea."

"Show her the symbol on the back," Sterling prompted.

Prince Eristan turned the document over and pointed out the strange emblem. He turned the parchment back over and then held it up to the light. "Look, you can see the symbol right through the parchment."

"I don't see it," his sister replied.

"Well, I can," Eristan told her. He studied the parchment. "That's strange."

Sterling leaned forward. "What is?"

"When you hold the parchment to the light, the symbol appears right over the word *city*, as if it was planned that way, and the arrow seems to be pointing to that word."

"I still don't see the symbol," Cordelia insisted.

"It's faint, but it's there," Prince Eristan replied. "Here, look." He held the parchment directly over the lamp, just inches from it, so that the light shone through the material. "See? You can see the symbol right through the parchment and it appears directly over the word *city*, almost as if to emphasize it."

"Oh, look!" Cordelia shrilled. As the three young people watched in stunned amazement, brown lines appeared on the parchment as if by magic. The lines appeared slowly, distinctly, as if drawn by an unseen presence in the room. Cordelia gave a little shriek and leaped back from the parchment. "What manner of sorcery is this?" she quavered.

Sterling laughed at her. "There's no sorcery about it, Cordelia. It's simply a form of invisible writing."

"Invisible writing?" The girl stared at the parchment and then back at Sterling, and her countenance betrayed the fact that she was considering bolting from the room.

"It's nothing to fear," he told her quietly.

"Then how did the letters appear?" Cordelia's voice trembled.

"There's nothing mystical about it. There are many ways to produce invisible writing, but the maker of this parchment probably used the juice from a lemon to form the letters. Once the juice dried, the writing was not visible until the heat from the lamp made it appear."

Cordelia looked at Eristan for assurance and then began to relax.

Three heads bent over the parchment as the young people studied the mysterious manuscript. The crude diagram was drawn in thin, spidery lines, so slight they appeared to have been written by a scribe barely able to touch the quill to the parchment.

"It *is* a map of some sort," Sterling declared, staring at Prince Eristan with a puzzled expression on his face.

"It looks like a map of one of the castles," the young prince replied. "Look, here's the outer curtain, the castle approach, the drawbridge—"

"All right, it's a castle," his friend agreed. "But which one? And why would a peasant be so determined to get it to you?"

Prince Eristan shrugged. "Who knows?" He frowned as he placed a finger on the document. "This is the main gate, the outer barbican, and the inner gate to the castle bailey—but someone has scribbled them out. Why are they obscured as if they don't exist?"

Sterling studied the map for a long moment as if he expected to find the answer upon the faded parchment. "Perhaps that part of the castle has been torn down. Or perhaps the person who drew this was planning an attack on the castle and wanted to indicate that this would not be the approach to take."

Cordelia spoke in a quiet voice, a barely audible whisper, as if afraid to speak aloud. "Which castle is it?"

"I've seen many of the castles of Cheswold," Sterling told her, "but I've never been to this one."

"In the city forbidden," the young princess read again, "doth the lion crouch deep. A treasure lies hidden, though far from the keep." She frowned and looked from Eristan to Sterling and then back to the parchment. "That's a strange verse, and an even stranger map." She looked from one companion to the other. "Do either of you have any idea what this means?"

"I'm sure we don't," her brother replied. "Though I think I'd give half the kingdom to know where it came from."

Chapter Seven

Prince Eristan sat quietly astride the tall, milk-white mare with his hunting bow resting against the pommel of the saddle. Sensing movement in the thicket just ahead, he carefully fitted an arrow to the bowstring and pulled to half-draw. Releasing his breath in a long, quiet sigh, he waited.

He tensed as he heard movement in the thick carpet of autumn leaves. The stag, if that's what it was, was moving directly toward him. Trembling with excitement, he took a deep breath, held it, and pulled to full draw. His heart beat with anticipation. At this range, he knew he couldn't miss. This was his first hunt, and he was about to take his first trophy.

"This one's mine," he whispered.

Sterling nodded once. "Aye."

Prince Eristan felt a surge of disappointment as a squirrel dashed from the thicket, crossed in front of the mare, and then scrambled up a thick maple. "Thanks, Sir Squirrel," he said quietly. "I thought for sure you were a trophy hart, for I was about to put an arrow through your heart." The squirrel scolded the two young huntsmen and then darted toward the treetops.

Sterling laughed. "It sounded like a hart, didn't it?"

Prince Eristan shook his head. "He certainly made enough noise." He relaxed the tension on his bowstring. "Let's ride back to the others."

Prince Eristan and Sterling rode down the side of the ridge, skirted a pond bordered with tall stands of cattails, and began to follow a trail that wound its way down into a narrow valley. "I think this takes us back to the road," Prince Eristan said to Sterling.

"So the coronation is this afternoon," Sterling remarked. "Are you ready? Oh, by the way, my best wishes for your birthday."

"Thanks," Prince Eristan replied. "Be sure to wish Cordelia the same when you see her."

"I will," his companion replied. "Are you ready for the coronation?"

The young prince shrugged. "I don't feel ready to be king, if that's what you're asking. I'm ready for the coronation, but not for the throne."

Sterling nodded to show that he understood. "You'll do well, Prince Eristan. Remember, you are the son of King William."

Prince Eristan sighed. "I hope that's enough. The one thing that worries me most is the Karnivans. How am I going to deal with them?"

"King William was known to be one of the greatest battle strategists of all time," his friend replied. "Perhaps you inherited that same ability."

The young prince sighed again. "Perhaps."

The young prince slowly became aware of another presence and turned in the saddle. His heart leaped. Moving through the brush less than fifteen yards away was a large hart with a tawny pelt and a tall set of antlers. The creature was upwind of the hunters and as yet had not sensed their presence. Holding his breath, Prince Eristan quietly slipped an arrow to the bowstring and pulled to full draw. The hart was moving directly toward him and seemed unaware of him, so the young hunter waited. If the hart would take just four or five more steps he would be out of the underbrush and Eristan could get a clear shot. The hart paused and turned directly toward him. Eristan's heart pounded.

The hart's head shot up and his entire body tensed at the sound of the staccato of hoof beats. In an instant, he whirled and darted away through the brush, gone as suddenly and silently as a phantom. Prince Eristan turned in the saddle and a cold thrill of fear surged through his chest. A score of mounted knights rode at full gallop up the narrow track and within seconds disappeared over the crest of the ridge. One glance told him the identity of the cavalcade of knights—Karnivans were easy to identify by their unique armor.

"Thank Emmanuel that they didn't see us," Sterling said quietly. "Let's get back to Sir Reginald and Lord Keidric."

"Karnivans!" Prince Eristan said in disgust. "What arrogance they show in riding this far from their border and this close to Barrington Castle."

"If they had seen us," Sterling remarked, "Cheswold would be looking for another king. Come on, Eristan, let's get out of here. We have to hurry back for the coronation, anyway."

The two young hunters turned their mounts and rode swiftly back the way they had come. "This just shows how crucial it is for us to secure our border," Eristan declared, "and to begin training our troops immediately. If Karnivan war parties are riding this close to Barrington Castle, no shire or castle in Cheswold is safe."

Moments later they rode into the glen where they had

last seen their hunting companions, Sir Reginald and Lord Keidric. Both men had dismounted and were down on their knees examining the carcass of a hart. "Who took him?" Prince Eristan asked.

Sir Reginald looked up with a wide grin. "Venture one guess."

Prince Eristan laughed. "Well done, Pa. He's a nice one."

As Eristan and Sterling watched, the two men lifted the carcass and placed it behind the saddle of Sir Reginald's horse. While Sir Reginald lashed it in place, Prince Eristan quietly told him about the Karnivan war party. Sir Reginald's face was grave. "The kingdom is in trouble, Eristan, deep trouble, unless we can move quickly to secure our borders and rebuild our armies."

"I intend to do both as hastily as possible," the young prince replied. "Pa, why did King Vladimir allow the kingdom of Cheswold to reach such a state?"

The man shrugged. "I cannot properly answer that question without better knowing King Vladimir. Hopefully, it was mere carelessness, and not intentional."

"Intentional, Pa?"

"King Vladimir is a puzzle to many. There are those who fear that Vladimir intended to yield the kingdom to Grimlor and merge Cheswold with Karniva."

"If that is what he intended, why has he not done so already?"

Sir Reginald hesitated. "I'm not saying that King Vladimir had such intentions at all, mind you, but if he did, I suppose that he would move slowly so that the populace would not rise up in rebellion against such an idea. I suppose also that he was being cautious in negotiating with a man like Grimlor."

Lord Keidric spoke up. "I, for one, fear that Vladimir did fully intend to yield the kingdom to Grimlor. Your coronation interferes with those plans, doesn't it?"

"But he's been on the throne for fourteen years!" Eristan protested. "Why would he not have accomplished such a purpose in that amount of time?"

Sterling glanced at the sun. "Prince Eristan, we had better get back to the castle. You don't want to be late for your own coronation."

Prince Eristan laughed. "That would not be a good way to start my reign, would it?"

Moments later, as the hunting party rode up the castle approach, they met Cordelia and two of her ladies-in-waiting. "Good morning, Cordelia," Sir Reginald greeted the young princess.

Princess Cordelia eyed the carcass on the back of the horse. "I see that you had a successful hunt, Pa. My congratulations." Teasingly, she looked at the rest of the hunting party. "I also see that Pa is the only one with a hart, for I see three hunters empty-handed."

Prince Eristan pretended to take offense at her words. "I'll have you know, Princess Cordelia, that we helped Sir Reginald make his kill."

Sterling gazed curiously at Princess Cordelia. "And just where have you and your ladies been?"

The princess looked from Sterling to Eristan and back again. "I have found the loveliest spot for solitude! My ladies and I have visited it frequently in the last few days. Come with me and I'll show you."

Eristan shook his head. "There isn't time. I don't want to be late for my own coronation."

Teasingly, Cordelia pretended to pout. "It will just take a minute or two. You won't be late." She grinned at him. "Come on."

Eristan shrugged as if to say that arguing with her was pointless. "Dismiss your ladies-in-waiting and you can double with me," he offered.

Moments later, Cordelia swung up behind Eristan's saddle. "Ride across the moor to the point where the woods are the thickest," she instructed.

Following Cordelia's directions, Prince Eristan and Sterling rode east from the castle and entered a densely wooded ravine. The horses fought their way through the thick undergrowth and then, abruptly, a trail opened before them. After following the trail for thirty yards, the horses emerged into a secluded glen.

Sterling and Prince Eristan looked about them in wonder. "Cordelia, this is incredible!" Eristan exclaimed softly.

The riders found themselves surrounded by a riot of color. Fiery red maples, golden tamarack and birch, orange sugar maples, purple ash, butter-yellow hickories—the glen blazed with the brilliant colors of autumn. Wildflowers grew in vivid profusions of color as if determined to outdo each other. At the upper end of the glen, a crystal stream tumbled over mossy rocks in a series of bubbling cataracts. A light breeze stirred in the treetops and a delightful fragrance wafted in the air.

"Most of the trees in Cheswold have started losing their leaves," Sterling commented, "but here it looks like the leaves are at their finest."

Prince Eristan sniffed the air. "It smells like honeysuckle."

"Too late in the year for honeysuckle," Sterling retorted.

"I know, but doesn't it smell like it? Cordelia, this place is paradise!"

"I love it here," the princess replied, dropping to a seat on a sandstone outcropping at the edge of the clearing. "My ladies-in-waiting and I have been coming here every day this week. I feel like it's a refuge from all the noise and bustle of the castle. I've never seen such a peaceful place."

Prince Eristan dismounted and strode over to the tumbling cascades, dipping his hand into the crystal waters. "I can see why you would want to come here often," he replied. "This is a peaceful place. If you don't mind, I may start coming here myself when the stress of ruling becomes too great for me."

He gazed around at the colorful foliage. "This glen is so magnificent that it needs a name. Something elegant. Something that would suggest a refuge from the noise and bustle of everyday life." He paused. "How about 'Solitude' for a name? What do you think?"

Cordelia shook her head. "I think I like 'Tranquility' better."

Her brother nodded. "Then 'Tranquility' it shall be."

Sterling glanced at the sun. "Prince Eristan, we had better get back to the castle."

Eristan laughed and nodded. "Let's ride." He swung into the saddle. Cordelia scrambled up after him and he turned the horse toward Barrington Castle.

The approach to the castle was a scene of noisy confusion. Crowds of peasants on foot chattered excitedly as they pushed and shoved their way toward the castle gates, eager to witness the grand coronation, while wealthy landowners, merchants, and nobility rode prancing horses or traveled in elegant carriages. At the same time, a double line of Cheswoldian soldiers marched from the castle, doing their best to keep rank as they pushed their way through the jostling crowds.

"Why are the soldiers leaving the castle?" Princess Cordelia asked, turning to Prince Eristan.

"They're to assemble on the parade grounds and march into the castle in a show of force to start the coronation proceedings," Eristan told her. "It was Lord Aric's idea." He reined to a slow walk as the horses approached the noisy throng. "King Vladimir and I are to sit on the balcony of the palace to review the troops. After that, Vladimir is to make a speech, officially relinquishing the throne to me, and then Lord Aric and the High Council will conduct the actual coronation ceremony." He shook his head in disbelief. "Just think, Cordelia, in less than two hours I will be the king of Cheswold. This whole thing is like an unbelievable dream, is it not?"

At that moment a mounted knight reined in beside Prince Eristan. "Lord Aric is looking for you, sire. The coronation ceremonies are about to commence."

The young prince nodded. "Take me to him."

Moments later Prince Eristan and Lord Aric stood just inside the balcony foyer, out of sight of the exuberant throng. Eristan peered out across the bailey. The vast courtyard was filled from one end to the other with jostling, chattering people. Peasants and nobility alike stood on tiptoe, faces upturned toward the balcony, each one eager for a glimpse of the youthful prince who was soon to be their new king.

Prince Eristan felt a soft hand in his and turned to see Princess Cordelia beside him. "Quite a robe you have there, Your Majesty," she said so softly that the prime minister could not hear. "Are those real gems?"

Eristan snorted as he glanced down at the glittering garment. "I'm afraid so. This thing must have cost a fortune."

Cordelia grinned at him. "Lord Aric's idea?"

"Right again. He wants to impress the populace with the wealth of Cheswold."

She eyed the elegant garment. "You could sell that and feed an entire city for a year."

The prime minister approached. "Are you ready, Your Majesty? It is time for Cheswold to welcome their new king!"

An attaché entered the foyer and hurried to address Lord Aric. "King Vladimir cannot be found, sire. We have searched high and low."

"Keep searching," Lord Aric ordered. The aide bowed and hurried from the room.

The prime minister snarled to show his impatience. "Where can he be? It is time for the ceremonies to begin." He sighed heavily. "King Vladimir is doing this deliberately." He turned to Eristan. "Would you care to have a seat, sire? It may be a few moments before we locate King Vladimir."

Lord Aric began to pace up and down, glancing out at the restless crowd from time to time and muttering under his breath. The minutes dragged like hours. The crowd in the bailey swelled until it seemed that the walls would explode outward from the press.

At last, the attaché hurried into the room. "The unthinkable has happened," he announced, looking from Prince Eristan to Lord Aric and then back again. "We have just learned that King Vladimir has left the castle, taking two army battalions with him. Sire, there is every indication that he plans to start a civil war."

Chapter Eight

Prince Eristan and Lord Aric stared at the attaché, stunned by the incredible message that he had just delivered. "A civil war?" the prime minister echoed. "Why would Vladimir do this? This is . . . unthinkable!"

Sir Reginald, Lord Keidric, and Lord Stephen hurried into the chamber at that moment. Reginald stepped close to Prince Eristan. "Son, there's trouble brewing," he said in a quiet voice.

Eristan nodded. "I know, Pa. Vladimir is possibly leading an insurrection. We just learned of it." He sighed heavily and looked from one man to another. "What course of action do we take now?"

Sir Reginald shrugged. "First of all, we proceed with the coronation as planned, with or without Vladimir. Your father decreed that you were to become the king of Cheswold upon your sixteenth birthday, and so it shall be. All of Cheswold awaits this moment and Vladimir shall not take it from them."

"The High Council has assembled in the anteroom," Lord Aric informed them, "and they shall conduct the coronation as planned." He glanced toward the castle gates. "Captain Orwyn and the troops are in place, well, three battalions of them, anyway. Let the ceremonies begin!"

At a gesture from Lord Aric, six heralds in bright vestures stepped forward and sounded a rousing fanfare on their trumpets. As the golden notes echoed across the crowded bailey, the army of Cheswold marched grandly through the gates and paraded proudly toward the palace. The crowds were in frenzy, cheering wildly and throwing hats and small articles of clothing into the air. Lord Aric nodded toward Eristan, who stepped out onto the balcony with the elegant robe gleaming brilliantly in the sunlight.

The crowd went wild. The lusty cheering became a roar that swelled in volume until it seemed that the palace trembled with the sound. Overwhelmed, Prince Eristan managed to wave to the throng before dropping to a seat on the elegant coronation throne. Led by Lord Wallace, the High Council marched ceremoniously onto the balcony, split into two groups, and stood stiffly at attention on both sides of the gallery. Bearing the crown of Cheswold on a satin cushion, Lord Aric stepped out onto the balcony.

Prince Eristan's heart pounded furiously and he realized with some dismay that he was trembling. This was his grand moment, the moment for which all Cheswold had been waiting since the death of his father, King William, and yet, he suddenly felt overwhelmed and fearful. *I am nothing but a peasant. How can I rule Cheswold?*

As Lord Aric stood stiffly at attention bearing the crown of Cheswold, Lord Wallace stepped to the railing and raised both hands to still the throng. It took nearly three minutes, but at last, a hush settled across the crowded bailey. "Good people of the kingdom of Cheswold," the magistrate began, lifting his powerful voice so that the sound rang throughout the bailey, "welcome to Barrington Castle and the grand coronation of our new king. Today is a proud and glorious moment in the history of our great nation."

A murmur of excitement swept across the crowd and the magistrate waited until it had subsided.

"Fourteen long years ago, our king, William of Cheswold, was killed in the battle for Barrington Castle. After the death of our beloved king, Vladimir of Stocklin was installed as regent and has served Cheswold in that capacity ever since. The High Council wishes to express our appreciation to Vladimir for his years of service to the realm."

Lord Wallace paused and swept the crowd with a glance.

"Before his death, King William had decreed that his only son, Prince Eristan, would ascend the throne upon his sixteenth birthday. Today marks the birthday of the prince, and we are assembled here to crown—"

At that point an enthusiastic roar from the crowd drowned out the magistrate's words and he was forced to pause until the cheering had subsided.

"Today we are assembled," Lord Wallace began again, "to crown Prince Eristan as our king, King Eristan of Cheswold. May his reign be long and glorious, and may he serve in the traditions of his father, King William of—" The cheering erupted again and the magistrate was forced to pause.

Lord Wallace continued his address for another twenty minutes, extolling the virtues of the young king, reminding the people just how fortunate they were to live under such a sovereign, and admonishing them to be loyal to the throne. After the magistrate finished his speech, one dignitary after another addressed the crowd so that the speechmaking continued for nearly two hours and became a wearisome affair.

Midway through the speeches, Eristan stifled a yawn and took a deep breath in an effort to stay awake. The elegant coronation robe was hot and stifling, and he struggled to keep his eyes open. He glanced at the crowd. *They're as tired of this as I am,* he realized. *One or two more speeches like this one and the whole kingdom will be asleep!* He stifled another yawn and turned his attention to a young peasant woman who stood fifty paces from the balcony. The woman had a young baby in her arms, and, as Eristan watched, she bounced the baby up and down in an effort to keep her quiet. *I'm tired of this whole affair,* the young king told himself, *but at least I am seated on a comfortable throne. These poor people have to stand!*

When at last the speeches were finished, a troupe of skilled musicians filed past playing the Cheswoldian anthem "May His Reign Be Long and Glorious" as the people cheered enthusiastically, in effect, drowning out the music. At last, the grand moment arrived. The six heralds in bright uniforms lifted their golden trumpets and sounded a long fanfare. As the powerful notes echoed across the crowded bailey, Lord Wallace stepped forward.

"Prince Eristan," he called in a sonorous voice that resonated across much of the bailey, "please step forward, sire." An attendant placed a velvet cushion upon the floor of the balcony so that Eristan stepped up on it.

Lord Wallace turned and took the crown from Lord Aric. "By the authority of King William, king of Cheswold, and King Vladimir, regent of Cheswold, I crown thee, Prince Eristan, as the new king of Cheswold. King Eristan, may your reign be long and glorious, and may your subjects live in—" The rest of his words were drowned out by the exuberant cheering of the crowd.

When order was restored, Lord Wallace made another short speech, followed by a speech by Lord Aric. The crowd grew restless.

At last, Lord Wallace dismissed the crowd to an afternoon of feasting and pageantry as King Eristan and his entourage made their way to the great hall of the palace for an elaborate banquet. The streets of Barrington were alive with music and dancing as the delicious smells of hot pies, spiced wines, and gingerbread wafted in the air. Musicians, jugglers, acrobats, and even trained animals performed in the streets to the delight of young and old alike. Peasants mingled with nobility as the kingdom of Cheswold celebrated the coronation of her new king.

Late that night, a crescent moon bathed Barrington Castle in a gentle silver light as huge snowflakes drifted down, silently covering the courtyard in a blanket of white. Young King Eristan stood at the railing of the balcony, intently gazing across the tranquil scene before him. The bailey was silent; the crowds were gone; and the pristine snow covered their tracks as if they had never been there. The castle walls gleamed silver and the new snow seemed to glow with a soft blue light.

The young king exhaled sharply and his breath hung in the air like a luminous silver cloud. Hearing the tiniest whisper of a noise, he turned, and jumped as Princess Cordelia's face appeared just inches from his own. She laughed softly. "I didn't mean to startle you."

He shrugged.

"You couldn't sleep, either?" Cordelia said.

Eristan shook his head. "My thoughts are in a maelstrom of confusion ever since the coronation this afternoon. Cordelia, I'm the king! The king of Cheswold! How am I to rule an entire nation when I don't know the first thing about governing a country? I wish Father was here."

She touched his hand. "King Emmanuel will guide you, and

you have some very capable counselors—Pa, and Lord Keidric, and Sir Stephen . . . and Melzar. These are all wise men, and they will be sources of good advice, I'm sure. You're not alone, Eristan."

He nodded. "The greatest threat to the kingdom of Cheswold, of course, is Grimlor and the Karnivans. What are we to do if they invade? Our army is in pathetic shape, Cordelia. The battalions are poorly trained and poorly equipped, and morale among the men is terrible. It seems that King Vladimir purposely withheld funds and training, almost as if he intended to weaken our forces. If the Karnivans attacked tomorrow, I'm afraid Cheswold would be wiped out."

Eristan sighed. "And then there's Vladimir. He took two battalions, you know. Two battalions. Nearly half the army is in his hands, and we really don't know what he is planning. Is he planning a coup to take back the throne? Is he planning to join forces with Grimlor? None of us has any idea what Vladimir intends, and that's what makes Cheswold so vulnerable. Cordelia, I'm the king and all of Cheswold will look to me for leadership, and yet I don't know how to protect my people."

Princess Cordelia was silent.

"Melzar will start training the troops first thing tomorrow morning—we'll waste no time doing that—and yet, what if that is not enough? What if Grimlor invades Cheswold before our soldiers are trained? What if Vladimir organizes a rebellion and attempts to retake the throne? What if—"

"Take it one day at a time, Your Majesty," the princess replied softly, brushing snow from her brother's shoulders. "Today the coronation went well. Tomorrow Melzar begins to train the troops. You and your advisors can begin to secure Cheswold's borders, plan defense strategies, maybe even place spies in Vladimir's ranks to discover his plans. But take it one day at a time." She smiled at him. "Right now, Your Majesty, you need to get some sleep."

King Eristan turned and gazed across the moonlit bailey as the snow continued to fall. "This task is much too big for me, Cordelia. I'm not ready to be king."

Cordelia took his arm and turned him toward the palace. "One day at a time, Your Majesty," she said quietly. "Let's get some sleep."

King Eristan and Sir Reginald strode briskly across the parade grounds of Barrington Castle. The three remaining battalions of the army of Cheswold were assembled, rank upon rank, all watching intently as a skirmish took place atop a high wooden platform in the center of the field. An old man and a stout captain were sparring furiously.

Captain Vance and Captain Trevarr approached the young king. "Your Majesty, the training exercises are going well," they reported. "Lord Melzar is incredible!"

King Eristan found it amusing that the captains had afforded the old man a title. "Melzar is not a lord," he replied, "just a commoner who is unusually skilled with a sword."

"Commoner or not, his battle skills are almost beyond belief," Captain Vance asserted. "At first glance, one would think him too old to even wield a sword, but in his hands, the weapon moves like lightning. The men are in awe of him, sire, as if he possesses some sort of supernatural powers."

"In just three days time, Your Majesty, Lord Melzar has taught the troops the defensive use of the sword more thoroughly and effectively than I would have thought possible. Morale has improved dramatically. The men come to the exercises eager to learn and excited about practicing their new skills. It's as if we have a whole new army, sire."

"Lord Melzar trains the officers each morning," the second captain said, "and the officers then train the troops in the afternoon. The plan has worked well, far better than we could have anticipated."

The young king was pleased. "Excellent, just excellent," he replied. "How are the plans progressing for the securing of our border?"

The demonstration skirmish had ended and the officers were shouting orders as they divided their troops into smaller units for practice. Sheathing his sword and wiping the sweat from his brow, Melzar approached King Eristan and his companions. "Training is progressing nicely so far, Your Majesty," he reported, bowing to Eristan. "The officers are throwing themselves whole-heartedly into this endeavor and the troops seem eager to learn."

"So I have heard," King Eristan replied. "Sir, I am grateful for your help with the training. I know of no one in Cheswold who could do this as effectively as you."

"I am happy to serve," the old man replied, bowing again as his eyes twinkled. "I am grateful for the opportunity, sire."

Eristan turned to find Lord Keidric at his elbow. "You're a man of war, Lord Keidric. What do you think of the troops' progress?"

The nobleman nodded approvingly. "We have a long way to go, of course, sire, but these three days of training have exceeded my greatest expectations. Lord Melzar is indeed a master swordsman and an outstanding teacher, and the officers and troops alike are responding well to him. Within weeks, Cheswold will have a new army."

"The two battalions at Vladimir's disposal will not have such training," Sir Reginald remarked. "Emmanuel be praised for that."

"We are in need of new weaponry, sire," one of the captains reminded the young king.

Eristan nodded. "We have nearly every smithy in the kingdom working on that," he replied. "Sir Reginald has men checking their work for quality of materials and workmanship. Even so, outfitting the troops may take longer than training them. I have also petitioned King Emmanuel, asking His Majesty to provide each man with his invincible sword."

"Sire, I would also suggest a new training project," Melzar said, "with your permission, of course."

King Eristan turned to him. "And what project is that, sir?"

"Cheswold is in need of a strong cavalry," the old man replied. "Our borders with Karniva are long and we need to have the ability to move men quickly to defensive positions. Such a thing is not possible with foot soldiers alone. We need to develop and train some cavalry units."

"Where would we get the necessary horses?" Captain Orwyn questioned.

"I am told that vast herds of wild Berkshire horses run free on the western plains of Cheswold," Melzar replied. "Berkshires make excellent warhorses—they're swift and strong; they respond well to training; and they have stamina such as no other breed possesses."

He looked around at the circle of men. "I propose that we send a team of men at once to western Cheswold to round up a remuda of three hundred horses and bring them to a location close to Barrington Castle for training. We could commission a team of carpenters to build barns and corrals even as the horses are being caught."

"Lord Melzar, who would break and train the horses?" Captain Orwyn asked.

"I am not a lord, sire," Melzar replied quickly, "just a commoner eager to serve my king and my country." For an instant he turned and surveyed the troops who were just beginning to skirmish with each other, and then turned back to face the young king. "I can help train the cavalrymen in swordsmanship, but I know not who would break and train the horses."

The men looked at each other. "Then we still need a horse trainer," Sir Reginald said. "We can't have a cavalry unit unless we have horses."

"I know just the man," Lord Keidric replied. "There is a hostler at Windstone Castle who trained warhorses for King William. Cheswold had a strong cavalry unit before Vladimir took the throne, but Vladimir disbanded it, saying that it was unnecessary."

"Would this hostler be up to the task of training three hundred warhorses in a short period of time?" Captain Orwyn asked.

Lord Keidric nodded. "Aye, with the help of a few assistants, he would. This man knows and understands horses like no other. I often accuse him of thinking like a horse."

"Then let us proceed with such a plan at once," King Eristan decided. He looked curiously at Lord Keidric. "Who at Windstone Castle has such ability with horseflesh? I do not know of such a man."

"You know him well, Your Majesty," Lord Keidric replied. "The man in question is none other than my stablemaster, Garven."

Chapter Nine

"Berkshires are grand animals, are they not?" Sir Reginald said in admiration, as he and King Eristan watched a score of powerful horses thunder across the snowy parade grounds of Barrington Castle. "Deep of chest, strong of limb, swift as eagles—they're magnificent, Eristan!"

The young king nodded. "Garven and his men chose the best of the best, did they not? Cheswold will soon have the finest cavalry in all Terrestria."

"Garven says that Berkshires train easily," Reginald remarked, watching intently as half a dozen mounted hostlers drove the galloping horses toward a waiting corral. "He hopes to start breaking them tomorrow."

Eristan nodded. "Pa, with Garven training our new horses and Melzar training the troops, I'd say that our army is in far better shape than it was three weeks ago when I became king. The troops still have a long way to go and we still need new weapons and uniforms, but we've made a lot of progress. I praise Emmanuel that Melzar was willing to undertake such a task. Pa, he's working from sunup to sundown each day."

"Quite a strenuous schedule for a man of his age," Sir Reginald agreed. He watched in admiration as the horsemen drove the remuda of wild horses into the corral, closing the gate behind them. "One thing is for sure—he knows what he is doing."

"I plan to give him a peytance of nobility once the training is complete and he has time enough to attend the ceremony," Eristan said. "He has served Cheswold well and I would like to honor him in that way."

"If I know Melzar, he won't accept it," Reginald said with a chuckle. "He's happy enough as a commoner and I don't think he has the least bit of interest in acquiring a title of nobility."

Eristan shrugged. "Aye, but be that as it may, I still wish to honor him in that way. I also would like to bestow some honor upon Miriam."

Sterling approached just then. "Sir Winston just rode from the castle in a rage, accompanied by half a dozen knights from the garrison. He was livid, Eristan, and he and his men looked as if they were plotting some mischief." He frowned. "What do you suppose has made Sir Winston so angry?"

"Yesterday was his last day as the constable of Barrington Castle," the young king explained. "This morning I installed Pa as the new constable. Sir Winston was quite put out, but he'll get over it."

Sterling shook his head. "I just hope he doesn't cause you grief."

Eristan shrugged. "I'm not worried about him. What can he and six men do?" He turned to two knights who stood a discreet distance away. "You men are dismissed. I won't need a bodyguard."

Just then one of the hostlers turned his mount and galloped toward them. As the man drew his horse to a stop and swung down from the saddle, King Eristan was surprised to see that it was Garven. The stablemaster swept his hat from his head, approached haltingly, and then dropped to one knee, bowing so low that his face rested on his knee. "Your Majesty."

"Rise, Garven," Eristan replied.

Garven obeyed, but stood trembling with his head bowed contritely. "My lord, I am grateful for a second chance."

"All is forgiven, Garven," Eristan told him. "The past is forgotten and we will not discuss it again, but I do expect you to show your loyalty by serving Cheswold and the crown faithfully."

"Your Majesty, it is an honor to serve you." Garven threw a cautious glance toward the corral where the newly caught horses wheeled and stamped restlessly. "Does Your Majesty approve of the new horses?" He looked at Eristan for the first time. "We were very careful in their selection, sire, taking only those that were the healthiest and the most spirited. We—we did our best, sire."

The young king nodded approvingly. "The horses are magnificent, sir. I have no doubt that you and your men selected only the very best."

The hostler looked relieved. "Within weeks, sire, Cheswold shall have the finest cavalry in Terrestria! My men and I shall begin breaking and training these new mounts this very evening." Again, he bowed low. "It is an honor to serve you, my lord, and I am grateful for your trust in me."

With these words, Garven dropped his gaze and walked back to his horse.

"Quite a change in Garven, is there not?" Sterling commented, as the trio strolled back into Barrington Castle. "He seems genuinely sorry for the way he treated you and Cordelia."

"His repentance does seem real enough," Sir Reginald replied. "Methinks that Garven will be a great asset to

Cheswold as we attempt to rebuild our armies and secure our borders against invaders."

As they passed through the inner castle gates, Sir Reginald pointed across the bailey. "What is taking place over there?"

In the center of the courtyard, nearly a score of workmen were gathered around a sturdy work wagon and were struggling to offload an item wrapped in oilcloth. Three thick ropes tied around the item passed over pulleys suspended from a heavy crossbeam on a makeshift hoist. More than a dozen men pulled steadily on the ropes, slowly lifting the item from the wagon as others steadied it.

"Must be quite heavy," Sterling observed. "Look how many men are on the ropes."

As they watched, the workmen carefully lowered the oilcloth-wrapped item to stand upright on a seven-foot marble pedestal. Several of the men placed their hands against the item as if to steady it as the ropes went slack. "What is it?" Sterling wondered aloud.

King Eristan shrugged nonchalantly. "They're merely installing some new statuary."

Sir Reginald studied Eristan's face, noticing that he seemed uneasy, as if he had something to hide. "I want to see it," he announced, striding forward. The workmen saw him coming and respectfully moved aside as he approached. Sir Reginald lifted the lower edge of the oilcloth, revealing a foot fashioned of lustrous gold. "A golden statue," he exclaimed, turning to Eristan. "Is it solid gold?"

The young king nodded. "We plan to unveil it tomorrow in a public ceremony. Wait until you see it, Pa. It's magnificent!"

A strange look crossed Sir Reginald's face. "Let me venture a guess—it's a life-sized image of a certain young king that I know."

Eristan nodded eagerly. "It was Lord Aric's idea. We also plan to place similar statues in all the major cities of Cheswold, but they'll be bronze, overlaid with gold, rather than solid gold. The one here in Barrington Castle will be discreetly guarded day and night, of course."

Sir Reginald frowned. "A solid golden statue of you, Son? That would have cost a fortune! What is the purpose?"

"As you know, Pa, I'm the youngest king to ever take the throne of Cheswold. Lord Aric wants to impress the populace with my grandeur so that they will follow me more readily. The court musician is writing ballads praising my magnificence and we plan to send minstrels throughout the kingdom to introduce the ballads to the people."

Sterling stared at him. "Gaither is writing ballads about *you?*"

Eristan shrugged. "Why not? I'm the king of Cheswold! Who else should they write ballads about? I want the people to see me as a great king, perhaps the greatest king in Cheswold's history."

Sir Reginald and Sterling looked at each other wordlessly.

King Eristan failed to see the looks of dismay that swept across the features of his companions. "It's all part of a campaign planned by Lord Aric to present a positive image among the populace," he explained, "If my people see me as a powerful, capable leader, they will follow me without hesitation. If they see me as weak or vacillating they will not revere me or follow me."

"What if they see you as young, arrogant, and egotistical?" Sterling muttered.

Eristan swung on him. "What did you say?"

Sterling shook his head. "Nothing. It doesn't matter."

"The royal herald is designing a new coat of arms for

me—three golden lions, taken from my father's coat of arms. Lord Aric says that three lions instead of just one will suggest that my reign will be the greatest in history." He smiled in anticipation. "Once completed, my coat of arms will be placed strategically on the castles and major buildings throughout Cheswold. Each castle will also fly my coat of arms on a standard positioned over the main gate."

He smiled smugly. "We have also commissioned Kencaid to paint a number of portraits of me, one for every castle in Cheswold. We plan to hang my portrait in the great hall of each castle."

Sterling frowned. "Eristan, your coronation robe must have cost hundreds of thousands of klorins, if not millions. You're placing a life-sized golden statue in Barrington Castle and gold-plated statues in the cities. Placards for the buildings and standards for the castles and portraits to hang in the great halls—these projects must be costing a fortune!"

"And at a time when Cheswold needs to spend as much as possible to improve her military strength," Sir Reginald added.

"My scouts tell me that there has not been a single Karnivan patrol spotted in Cheswold in more than a fortnight," the young king replied. "Perhaps the danger from Grimlor and the Karnivans was overstated."

"Eristan, who is paying for all this?" Sterling stood before his friend with his hands extended.

"It's coming from the royal treasury," the young king replied calmly.

Sir Reginald laid a hand on his shoulder. "Outfitting your armies properly will cost a fortune, possibly more than there is in the royal treasury at this time. And with the threat of an invasion by the Karnivans, that should be top priority. Son, what if you don't have the funds to properly equip the troops?"

King Eristan's anger was beginning to boil. "We'll have the funds," he snapped. "We plan to raise taxes."

"Your people are struggling as it is," Sir Reginald retorted. "I think you need to realize that they may not be able to bear the burden of additional taxes."

"We won't raise the taxes on the poor," Eristan replied, "just on the wealthy—the nobility and the landowners."

"Increasing the taxes on the wealthy will affect the poor," Sir Reginald argued. "If you raise the amount of tax that a landowner must pay, he will simply demand more from the peasants who work his fields. If a merchant has to pay more taxes, he will charge more for his goods. Heavy taxes on the rich will also affect the poor."

"Most of your plans are extravagant and unnecessary," Sterling told him. "Cheswold would be best served by allocating more funds to strengthen your armies in defense against Grimlor and the Karnivans rather than erecting golden statues in the cities and hanging your portrait in the castles."

"I'll remind you that I am the king of Cheswold," Eristan said curtly. "I'll decide what's best for Cheswold, thank you."

"Eristan, the crown has changed you," Sir Reginald said sadly. "Perhaps it is true that power corrupts. When you took the throne just weeks ago you saw yourself as unworthy to rule Cheswold. You were humble. You thought of yourself as a commoner and saw yourself as being incapable of serving as king. You were ready to listen to advice and eagerly sought the counsel of men older and wiser than yourself."

He paused. "Now, after just weeks on the throne, it seems that you are impressed by your own glory and grandeur and cannot wait to impress your people with the same. It seems to me that everything that you and Lord Aric have planned is for the purpose of promoting yourself. Eristan, may I remind you that pride has been the downfall of many a king before you."

"Lord Aric says that I have the potential to become the greatest king in Cheswold's history," Eristan retorted. "He says that perhaps one day I shall become known as the king of all kings."

Sir Reginald's face showed his dismay. "King of kings—Eristan, that is a title reserved for King Emmanuel himself! No other king in all Terrestria will ever deserve that title."

"I—I won't use that title," the young king replied hastily. "But my plans for the kingdom still stand. The people of Cheswold will soon recognize the majesty of their king."

Sir Reginald sighed. "Son, the crown and the throne are not about you. As king of Cheswold, your greatest desire should be to serve King Emmanuel, and thereby serve the people of Cheswold. You may not see yourself as such, but as the king, in reality you are a servant. Only as you become a great servant will you truly become a great king."

"Pa, you speak in empty riddles," Eristan retorted angrily. "Whoever heard of a king becoming great by becoming a servant? The very idea does not make sense."

"The greatest king in all the history of Terrestria is King Emmanuel," the nobleman replied softly. "No one can argue with that. And yet, in all his splendor and majesty, Emmanuel was the greatest servant of all time."

King Eristan shrugged. "The statue will be unveiled tomorrow," he said flatly. "Plan to attend the ceremony or plan to stay away—it matters not to me."

Chapter Ten

King Eristan paused in the roadway and pried a rock out of his shoe. "I haven't walked this far since Sterling, Cordelia and I fled Windstone Castle and made the journey to Ainranon. Tell me again—why did you insist that we travel as peasants?"

"You're the king of Cheswold," Sir Reginald pointed out. "You don't have to make this journey unless you so desire."

"I'm also your adopted son," Eristan replied. "For nearly fourteen years I was taught to obey you." He grinned. "I'm not about to start disobeying now."

Sir Reginald laughed. "I want you to see again how the peasants live; therefore, we will travel as peasants so that we are not recognized. People act quite differently when they realize that they are in the presence of the king."

"Pa, I know how the peasants live," the young king responded. "We lived as peasants for fourteen years, did we not?"

The nobleman sighed. "All right, I'll tell you the whole of it. I want you to see the effect that your new, higher taxes are having on the peasants. You claimed that you were merely increasing the taxes on the rich, that the poor would be unaffected. I want you to see just what effect the higher taxes have had on the vast majority of your poorest subjects."

"Then you deceived me."

"Nay, not at all," the other man countered. He glanced at the sun. "Today is the first of the month. Many of the landlords collect their rents today, and that is what we have come to observe."

Eristan pointed. "There's a little farm up ahead. Perchance we can stop and ask for a drink. This is rugged country, and I've worked up quite a thirst."

His companion nodded. "Aye, of course."

Just ahead, a tiny shack nestled at the base of the mountain. Two scrawny goats foraged in the yard while a handful of chickens scratched here and there for worms and grubs. As Sir Reginald and Eristan approached the rude dwelling, a friendly voice hailed them. "Aye, and a good day to you, my friends. What brings you here?"

Eristan shielded his eyes against the sun and looked up. A thin peasant in his thirties was up on the thatched roof, kneeling at the edge, and carefully placing thatch across a crude framework of narrow poles that had been fastened to the side of the shack. "Greetings to you, my friend," Sir Reginald answered cheerily. "Would you be so kind as to spare two thirsty travelers a draught of water?"

"Aye, of course." The peasant crawled to the forward corner of the roof and then swung down to land beside them. "Just passing through, are you?"

Sir Reginald nodded. "Aye."

Two ragged children appeared at the corner of the house. "Micah, bring some water for these good men," the man said, addressing the eldest child.

The boy's eyes lit up as if he saw such a request as an honor. "Aye, Papa," he replied, darting eagerly into the house. In a moment he reappeared with a worn bucket and a gourd dipper. Drawing a dipperful of water from the bucket, he handed it to Sir Reginald. "This will slake your thirst, sire."

Sir Reginald offered the dipper to Eristan, who refused it. "You first, Pa."

The nobleman lifted the dipper and took a long, satisfying drink, completely emptying the vessel. As he handed it back to the boy, the staccato of hooves drew attention to the rutted lane leading to the shack. The youth's eyes widened in fright. "Pa, it's Sir Ralson!"

The man took the dipper from him. "Into the house," he said. "Don't worry about a thing." Micah took one more long, worried look at the approaching horsemen and then swept his little sister up in his arms and hurried into the shack.

Reginald leaned close to Eristan. "Sir Ralson is steward to Lord Alban of Chadwick. His companion is Sir Derrick, one of the knights of the castle garrison."

The two horsemen were elegantly dressed, armed, and wearing shirts of chain mail. As they drew their mounts to a stop, one called, "Landon, it's the first of the month."

"I know, sire," the peasant replied, and his shoulders sagged with the words as he dropped the dipper into the bucket. "Times are hard, sire, your lordship has to admit that, and lately it's been hard to come up with three klorins a month."

The steward laughed. "My friend, the rent is now five klorins."

"Five?" The peasant was stunned by the words. "Sire, it's all I can do to pay three klorins. There's no way I can possibly come up with five. Why the big increase, sire? This is rather sudden."

The horseman shrugged. "Our wretched king has raised our taxes and the money has to come from somewhere."

"Please give me more time, sire."

The steward's face was hard. "Are you saying that you don't have the money?"

"I'll have it soon, sire. Please give me another week."

"A week from now it will be eight klorins," the man replied. "And you'll work an extra day at the manor."

The peasant's face fell. "I work at the manor three days a week as it is, sire, and barely have time to work my own little field."

The steward snorted. "Do you think I should just let this go? Do you think I should let you pay whenever you feel like it? The rent is due today, Landon, and if you don't pay it, there has to be a late penalty." His eye fell upon the half-finished awning. "What are you building?"

"Just a bit of a goat shed, sire, just a sun shade, really. It's nothing, sire, just a place for my wife to milk the goats. And a place for them to get out of the rain if they have a mind to, sire."

Sir Ralson nodded approvingly. "It's good to see you making improvements, Landon. You're an industrious man, and that's good." He glanced slyly at his companion and then turned back to the peasant farmer. "The goat shed will cost you an extra klorin a month. Your rent is now six klorins a month."

"Six, sire?" Landon seemed to wilt at the words. "I—I'll never make it, sire. There is no way I can pay six klorins a month." Without thinking, he grabbed the steward's stirrup. "Sire, I'm begging you—"

"Never touch my horse!" Sir Ralson snapped, drawing his foot from the stirrup and kicking Landon's hand away. "We'll be back in a week. Either have nine klorins ready or vacate the property. And remember, you owe me an extra day at the manor." Wheeling their horses impatiently, the two men rode from the property.

Landon was distraught. "Nine klorins! What am I going

to do? I couldn't come up with that kind of money if I had a month, but they'll be back in a week."

"What are we going to do, Father?"

The farmer shook his head. "I don't know, Son, I don't know."

A slender woman with flaming red hair slipped from the shack just then and slipped her hand into his. Landon glanced at her. "Did you hear Sir Ralson?"

She nodded. "I heard the whole thing. What are we going to do, my love?"

Landon shook his head and drew his wife close to him. "I wish I knew, my sweet, I wish I knew."

Micah stood beside his parents and threw his thin arms around both of them. "Father, what will Sir Ralson do if we don't have the money next week?"

The peasant sighed, and he suddenly looked very old and very tired. "There's no telling, my son. He can throw us off Lord Alban's land if he wants. I really don't know what he will do."

"Where will we go if he throws us off the farm?"

"I really don't know, Son." The words were spoken so softly that Eristan could barely make them out.

Sir Reginald turned to Eristan. "You increased the taxes on the landowners and the wealthy," he said quietly, "and you assured me that it would not affect the poor. Do you still believe that?"

The young king didn't answer. Sir Reginald reached down, filled the dipper with water, and handed it to Eristan. "Son, here's the drink you were wanting." Eristan drank deeply, grateful for the cool water. When the dipper was empty, he handed it back to Reginald.

"More?"

Eristan shook his head.

As Sir Reginald returned the dipper to the bucket, Eristan heard the dull clink of metal against wood. "Thank you for the water, sir," he told Landon. "We need to be on our way, as we have quite a journey ahead of us."

The peasant nodded without speaking.

As the travelers walked back down the lane, Eristan turned to Sir Reginald. "What did you put in the bucket? I heard the sound of metal."

Sir Reginald shrugged. "Ten klorins. The peasant and the boy will find it before long, but they won't have to thank us effusively, for we won't be there."

An hour later they found themselves approaching a small city. "Let's see if there is an apothecary shop," Sir Reginald suggested, "so I can get some oil of peppermint for my sore throat."

"There's an apothecary," Eristan said a moment later, as he recognized the sign over the door of a tiny shop. A small bell tinkled as they entered. As their eyes grew accustomed to the dim light, they saw a woman with an infant and a small child talking with a tall, thin man. A small vessel sat on the table before them.

"Are you sure the ointment is that much?" the woman asked, with a look of despair. "That's twice as much as you charged me last week."

"I had to raise the price," the apothecary told her regretfully. "I'm sorry, really I am. Our new king has raised our taxes and I had to raise my prices as a result. I'm sorry."

The woman stared at two small coins in her hand. "But my John needs the ointment for his foot ulcers," she replied quietly, and her lip quivered. "I don't have enough money."

The man gave her a sympathetic look. "I'm sorry, really I am. But with these new, higher taxes, I'm barely making it myself. I told my wife just last night that I may have to close my shop."

The woman sighed as she blinked back tears. "Aye, well, thank you anyway. I'll have to figure something out." Sorrowfully, she left the shop.

"How can I help you?" the apothecary said, turning his attention to Eristan and Sir Reginald.

"I need some oil of peppermint for a sore throat," Sir Reginald told him.

"Aye, just the thing," the man said cheerfully, as he prepared a mixture in a small bowl. "That will be a klorin and a bob. I'm sorry that it has to be so much, but that new king of ours raised the taxes and it's hurting everybody." He sighed. "I wish I could have the chance to speak with His Majesty—I'd beg him to reconsider."

He smiled at Eristan. "Lad, what do you think of our new king? He's just about your age, I hear."

Eristan shrugged. "He hasn't been on the throne long. I haven't made up my mind yet."

"Well, I wish he could see how his new, higher taxes are affecting his subjects," the man grumbled. "He lives in his huge, elaborate palace, drinking from golden goblets and feasting on pheasant while his subjects starve. I heard tell that he is erecting golden statues of himself in all the cities. Imagine a statue made of solid gold! Such a thing would feed an entire city for a year."

The apothecary carefully spooned his concoction into a small vial. "If King Eristan could see how you and I live, maybe he'd reconsider and make life a bit easier for us common folk, don't you think? But he sits up there in his magnificent palace in Barrington, living a life of luxury, and I suppose he has no idea how his people live. Commoners like you and me are starving while King Eristan lives in wealth and splendor."

He looked at Eristan. "Am I right, lad?"

The young king shrugged. "I suppose so, sir."

Sir Reginald paid the apothecary, took his oil of peppermint, and together he and Eristan left the shop to the tinkling of the little bell. "Well, we're seeing that for which we came," the nobleman commented. "You're witnessing first hand just how the new taxes are affecting the poor of Cheswold. What do you think now?"

King Eristan was silent.

"Son, you didn't come to the throne to serve yourself, to live a life of selfish luxury, or to impress the people with your wealth and grandeur. You were entrusted with the crown so that you might serve King Emmanuel by serving others. Your father was great because he served the people. King William will go down in history as one of the greatest kings in Terrestria. The people loved him, for he dearly loved the people and did his best to meet their needs. You wouldn't find him living in luxury while his people suffered."

"He certainly lived in a magnificent palace," Eristan replied tersely.

Sir Reginald turned to face him. "The palace at Barrington Castle? Your father never lived there."

Eristan frowned. "What do you mean?"

"Barrington Palace was built after your father's death. King Vladimir had it built for himself. That's why the army of Cheswold is in such a deplorable state—the monies needed for uniforms and equipment went to the construction of the palace instead."

"Vladimir built it?"

"Aye. He chose a life of luxury at the expense of his people and his nation. Vladimir cared nothing for Cheswold or its people." He cleared his throat. "Your father was a servant to King Emmanuel, and therefore to the people, while Vladimir was a tyrant who cared only for himself. At this very moment Vladimir may be planning a civil war in an attempt to retake the throne, even though such a move would devastate Cheswold and possibly cause us to fall into the hands of Grimlor."

He opened the vial and sniffed the contents. "Young King Eristan, you must choose which king you will emulate. If you choose a life of selfish luxury at the expense of your subjects, you will become like Vladimir. If you choose to serve your people, and thereby serve King Emmanuel himself, you will be like your father, King William. The choice is yours."

The staccato of hoof beats caught their attention and they spun around just in time to see two horsemen bearing down upon them. Leaping headlong to the side of the road, they barely managed to avoid being trampled. Eristan picked himself up from the weeds and dusted himself off. "Fools!" he raged. "Little did they know that they nearly ran down their king!"

"Sir Ralson and his companion again," Sir Reginald replied. "They saw us as peasants, Eristan, and peasants don't matter, remember?"

Moments later the two horsemen turned their mounts into a narrow lane just two or three furlongs ahead. "They're going to Jacob's farm," Sir Reginald said urgently. "Hurry!"

Quickening their pace, the two travelers soon turned into the narrow lane and hurried toward a humble sod dwelling. As they approached the yard, Sir Ralson was leading a young boy toward his own horse while a man, woman, and four children stood weeping. The youth's hands were tied in front of him. "Please!" the woman cried, running to Sir Ralson and seizing his doublet. "He's just a boy! Please don't take him!"

Sir Ralson struck her hands down and thrust her from him. "I've been more than lenient," he snarled angrily. "This is the second month you have failed to pay. Your son now belongs to us. Perhaps in another year or two you can save enough to buy him back."

"Have pity on us," the father pleaded. "I was sick for several weeks and unable to take my harvest to market. We'll pay you as we can."

"And when will that be?" the landlord asked scornfully. "It's too late for mercy, Jacob. The lad now belongs to us."

Sir Ralson's captive was attempting to appear brave but his eyes betrayed him, revealing the fear that he was experiencing. His mother let out a wail of despair. "Please, sire, we're begging you! Return our son to us—he's just a lad—and we will be sure to pay you all."

Sir Ralson turned to the lad. "Mount up," he said gruffly.

"Ralson, release the lad," Sir Reginald ordered, striding forward.

"What?" Sir Ralson spun around. "Peasant, were you addressing me?" His tone was incredulous.

"I am Sir Reginald of Orwyn and I will pay you whatever this farmer owes you," Reginald said curtly. "Release the lad."

Sir Ralson hesitated for a moment and then abruptly drew his sword. "Stand clear, peasant. I know not who you are or what you seek, but you will not meddle in my affairs. I warn you, stand clear."

In an instant Sir Reginald drew a broadsword from within his robe. "I am Reginald of Orwyn, constable of Barrington Castle and guardian of His Majesty, King Eristan. Sir, I assure you, you do not want to cross swords with me. As I already told you, I will pay the debt owed by this man. I say again, release the lad."

Sword ready, Sir Ralson advanced slowly, warily. With a wild cry he abruptly leaped forward, swinging his sword in a vicious cut intended to take off Sir Reginald's head. Reginald calmly deflected the blow. Swords clanged as the steward advanced on Reginald, cutting, slashing, and thrusting with a ferocity that amazed Eristan. Reginald gave way just a step or two and then stood his ground, calmly giving blow for blow as he deflected the attack.

Eristan watched from a safe distance and within seconds realized that his adopted father was apparently in no real danger. Reginald was simply countering Ralson's assault, fighting in a defensive stance, but not pressing an offensive even when he had several opportunities to do so. After a few moments, the steward was panting with exertion, but Sir Reginald stood quietly, calmly parrying every move of his opponent's blade.

"Don't just stand there, Derrick!" the steward cried. "Do something!"

Roaring furiously, the Chadwick knight unsheathed his sword and charged into the fray. Eristan drew his own sword and rushed to Sir Reginald's aid. In an instant he found himself face to face with Sir Ralson. "Insolent pup!" the steward raged, swinging his sword in a murderous horizontal cut. "Dare you stand against me?"

The long hours of training with Melzar paid off. In a flash, the young king leaped to one side, averting the blow, and then with both hands brought his sword down upon the steward's sword arm. But for the chain mail, Sir Ralson would have lost an arm. As it was, the force of the blow struck the arm down, causing the blade of the sword to strike the ground and jolting the weapon from his hand.

"I yield!" the steward cried, with astonishment written across his features. His sword lay two paces away but he made no move to retrieve it. "Surrender, Derrick!" he called to his companion. "They have the better of me." Derrick lowered his sword.

"How much does Jacob owe you?" Sir Reginald asked, lowering his own sword and reaching into his robe. "Release the lad immediately and I will pay off his father's debt."

"Twenty klorins," Sir Ralson puffed, struggling to catch his breath.

"No late charges," Sir Reginald asserted. "How much?"

"Sixteen, then," the steward panted. As Derrick untied the boy's hands, Reginald counted out the coins. Moments later, the two men mounted their horses and rode from the farm.

"How can we thank you, sire?" the peasant farmer asked, as his eyes filled with tears. "But for you, our son would now be a slave to Lord Alban."

"I am thankful that we were here and could meet this need," Sir Reginald replied simply. "When the sun sets this evening your family can praise King Emmanuel that your son is still with you and that your debt is paid."

After saying their good-byes, Sir Reginald and King Eristan left the farm and began the long walk back to Barrington Castle. "As you saw today," Reginald told the young king, "the peasants and landowners alike will suffer under the higher taxes. You're their king, and you alone have the power to help families like those we saw today. I won't say any more about it, Son, but please think long and hard about what you have seen today."

Eristan didn't reply and was silent for most of the trip back to the castle.

As King Eristan and Sir Reginald walked across the drawbridge and passed into Barrington Castle, Melzar came hurrying to meet them. "Thank Emmanuel that you have come at last," he blurted, seizing both of Eristan's hands in his. "It's Princess Cordelia—she's been taken!"

"Taken?" Eristan echoed. "Taken where? By whom?" A cold knot of fear tightened within his chest.

"Princess Cordelia was abducted two hours ago by a band of armed men," the old man answered, as his eyes filled with tears. "We have reason to believe that she is in the hands of Vladimir."

Chapter Eleven

Silence reigned in the great hall at Barrington Castle as King Eristan stared at Lady Malta, Princess Cordelia's lady-in-waiting. At last he spoke. "You're certain that it was Vladimir's men that abducted Princess Cordelia?"

"Aye, Your Majesty," Lady Malta replied nervously. "There is no doubt in my mind. They were Vladimir's men."

"You're certain that they were not Karnivans."

"Nay, sire, they were not Karnivans."

"What makes you so certain?"

"Their horses were Cheswoldian, sire, as well as their armor and weapons. And the leader wore Vladimir's coat of arms."

"The coat of arms could have been a ploy. Perhaps they were Karnivans disguised as Cheswoldians."

The woman shook her head. "Nay, sire, for their leader was Captain Randor. He has a very distinctive gray mare with a slash of white across the neck. And he sits his saddle in a very unusual manner. I'd know him anywhere."

"How many men were there?"

"About a score, sire."

"Were they wearing armor?"

"Not full plate armor, sire." She paused. "If I remember

correctly, sire, they were wearing chain mail hauberks, gauntlets, and helmets."

"Tell us again what happened," Sir Reginald requested. The magistrates of the High Council leaned forward eagerly, as did the members of King Eristan's cabinet.

"Princess Cordelia and I went to Tranquility to admire the waterfalls," Lady Malta began, and her lips trembled as she recalled the incident. "They're all frozen, sire, as beautiful as sculptures of crystal. When we reached the glen, we dismounted and left our horses at the edge of the woods. As we walked down to the falls, a band of armed men swept down upon us. Two men dismounted, snatched the princess, and lifted her bodily onto one of the horses." Malta's eyes brimmed with tears. "They shoved me to the ground, sire, and rode off with her."

"Your Majesty, my men and I checked the scene," Captain Vance spoke up. "The band of men approached the glen from the east, forded the stream, and waited in ambush behind the outcroppings of granite downstream from the falls. We estimate that they waited approximately two hours before the princess was taken."

"So this was planned in advance," Sir Reginald commented.

Captain Vance nodded. "It certainly seems that way, sire. My very best trackers are following them right now, but we estimate that Vladimir's men have at least half an hour head start."

"How would they have known that Cordelia frequents Tranquility on a regular basis?" King Eristan asked. "Very few knew about that."

Lady Malta's eyes widened and she suddenly blurted, "Oh!"

Eristan looked at her. "Was there something else?"

The woman nodded. "I almost forgot, sire." She gave a nervous laugh. "This might be one of the most important details. One of the riders was Sterling."

"Sterling?" Eristan stared her in disbelief. "Sterling? Do you mean my friend, Sterling?"

She nodded. "Aye."

"Lady Malta, you must be mistaken. Why would Sterling assist Vladimir's men in the capture of Princess Cordelia? That just doesn't make sense."

"I'm almost certain that it was Sterling, sire," Lady Malta answered defensively. "He wore a helmet like the others, but he was the last rider and as he rode past, he lifted his visor and looked directly at me. I saw his face clearly. As he rode past, he held one finger to his lips as if to signal me not to call out." She took a deep breath and let it out slowly. "I'm almost certain that the last rider was Sterling, sire."

"That could explain how Vladimir's men knew to find Princess Cordelia at the glen," Lord Wallace suggested.

Eristan shook his head. "Why would Sterling betray me? Why would he betray Cheswold? Why would he betray Princess Cordelia? This just doesn't make sense at all. This is not the Sterling I know."

Sir Reginald approached Lady Malta. "Is it possible, my lady, that you could be mistaken? Could you have seen a knight that simply looked like Sterling?"

She shook her head. "It all happened so fast that I cannot be certain of anything, sire, but I'm almost certain that the rider was Sterling. He raised his visor as if he wanted me to see his face. He looked at me as if he knew that I would recognize him. And he signaled me so that I would not call out to him. It was almost as if he was trying to convey a message, sire."

She took a deep breath. "The more I think on it, sire, the more certain I am that it was indeed Sterling."

Eristan sighed and looked at Sir Reginald. "You know

Sterling fairly well, Pa. Is this possible? Could Sterling have played a part in Cordelia's abduction?"

Lord Keidric spoke up. "If Sterling has joined Vladimir's forces, he could do us irreparable harm. He knows too much. He knows exactly how we are training the troops; he knows our plans for securing the borders; he knows the weaknesses in our defenses. We have kept nothing from him."

"My son would never betray Cheswold," Lord Stephen declared. "Your Majesty, he would never betray you. You saved his life at Windstone Castle! Do you think he would repay you by arranging the abduction of your sister? As Sterling's father I can assure you, he would do nothing to jeopardize the kingdom, and he certainly would do nothing to hurt you or Princess Cordelia."

"Times change and people change," a magistrate replied. "Perhaps Vladimir made him an offer he couldn't refuse."

The nobleman bristled at the remark. "My son is as loyal to the crown as any one of you," he growled. "You do him a discredit to even suggest otherwise." He glared at the magistrate. "One day you will regret those words, sir."

"Please don't take offense at my suggestion, sire," the magistrate replied evenly. "This is a time of national emergency and we need to explore all possibilities. I for one do not believe that Sterling would have done this, and yet we need to consider it as a possibility. Forgive me if the idea offends you."

Melzar spoke up. "Sterling did not have a part in this. Methinks he rides with Vladimir's men in order to find a way to rescue the princess."

"You say that quite emphatically, sire," Sir Reginald said. "You seem quite certain."

Melzar nodded. "I am. I've known Sterling for just a short while, but I know him well enough to know that his loyalty is to Cheswold and to King Eristan. He would not have aided

Vladimir in the abduction of Princess Cordelia."

"And yet Lady Malta is quite certain that she saw Sterling riding with the abductors," one of the magistrates reminded.

"Lady Malta is not completely sure that the rider was Sterling. She could be mistaken as to his identity. And if she is correct and Sterling was riding with Vladimir's men, there has to be a good reason for it. I really think he is looking for an opportunity to rescue Cordelia. I say again—Sterling is loyal to the crown and therefore would not have played a part in Princess Cordelia's abduction."

King Eristan looked at his advisors. "We can discuss Sterling later. Right now we need to figure out how to rescue Cordelia. It goes without saying that we should take no measures that would jeopardize her life."

"I suggest that we start by sending a petition to King Emmanuel," Sir Reginald said soberly. "His Majesty knows where Cordelia is at this very moment and he can guide us to her. He can keep her safe, even if she is in Vladimir's hands. We don't know whether or not Vladimir has her, and if so, what he intends to do with her. We must trust her safekeeping to Emmanuel."

Melzar produced a parchment and handed it to Eristan. "Your Majesty, perhaps you should be the one to send the petition."

Eristan accepted the parchment, took a quill, and began to write:

"Your Majesty, King Emmanuel,
As you already know, my Lord, Princess Cordelia has been taken from us and we do not know her whereabouts or how to safely conduct a rescue effort. We ask that you would protect Cordelia and keep her from harm. We ask that you would guide us as we plan a rescue.
Your son,
Eristan."

Rolling the parchment tightly, the young king raised his hand and released the document. In an arc of silver-blue light, the petition shot from his hand and vanished through the wall of the great hall. "My petition is now in the hands of His Majesty," he said with satisfaction. He turned to Captain Vance. "Let's take a full battalion and pursue the raiders at once," he ordered. "If we can overtake them tonight we can have Cordelia back at Barrington Castle before sunrise."

"Nay!" Melzar said.

Frowning, King Eristan turned to him.

"That may be exactly what Vladimir wants," Melzar replied. "There's less than half an hour until sunset and we can never overtake them before dark. If we attempt a rescue tonight the risks to Princess Cordelia will be too great. It would be better to wait until we get word from our trackers as to where Cordelia was taken and exactly who has taken her. We can then plan a rescue operation."

"Do you know how hard it is to sit here doing nothing while my twin sister is in the hands of Vladimir's men?" King Eristan growled. "I won't rest until she is safely back in Barrington Castle."

"Neither will we, Your Majesty," Melzar said quietly.

Eristan turned to Sir Reginald. "What do you think, Pa? Should we ride tonight in an attempt to overtake Vladimir's men and rescue Cordelia, or should we wait as Melzar is advising?"

"I would agree with Melzar," Reginald replied. "Son, it would be extremely difficult to track and overtake them in the dark, and a nighttime rescue attempt could endanger Cordelia's life. I would agree that it would be better to wait until we know for sure where Cordelia has been taken and exactly who we are dealing with."

"What if he plans to take her to Karniva and turn her over

to Grimlor?" Eristan replied. "If we pursued them tonight, perhaps we could intercept them and prevent that."

"If that is the case, we could never hope to overtake them before they reached the Karnivan border," Captain Vance replied.

"You said that you put four trackers on their trail," Eristan said, turning to the captain. "Four men could very easily walk into an ambush. That would allow Cordelia's abductors to get away cleanly. I want you to take one unit from your battalion and pursue the abductors, but do not engage the enemy unless you know Cordelia's whereabouts and can secure her safety. Be discreet and follow from a distance. Once you learn the whereabouts of the princess, send a rider back to Barrington Castle."

Captain Vance bowed. "As you wish, Your Majesty. We will ride at once."

"Captain."

"Your Majesty?"

"Your first concern is Cordelia's safety, Captain. Make certain that your men know that."

"Aye, Your Majesty. We will be mindful, sire. We will ride at once, sire." With a nod to the rest of the assembly, the officer hurried from the room.

King Eristan and his advisors discussed Princess Cordelia's abduction for the next twenty minutes, conjecturing as to the identity of her captors and weighing their options for a rescue attempt. Apprehension was written on each face and Eristan knew that the men were nearly as distressed as he. *These men are loyal to me and to Cheswold,* he thought gratefully. *We are in this together.*

At that moment a sentry hurried into the great hall. "A peasant has requested an audience with you, sire," he said to King Eristan. "He insists that he has a message from Vladimir."

Chapter Twelve

Silence again reigned in the great hall as a trembling peasant was led before King Eristan and the court. The man sank to his knees in obeisance fifteen paces from the young king. "Stand to your feet, my good man," Eristan ordered, "and tell us your name."

"My name is Peyton," the peasant replied, timidly standing up and lowering his gaze to the floor.

"What business do you have with me?" the king demanded.

"J-just moments ago, I—I was given five klorins to deliver a message to you, sire." The peasant extended a trembling hand, in which he clutched a rolled parchment. "Your Majesty, the message is from King Vladimir."

Sir Reginald extended his hand as he stepped between Eristan and the peasant. "I will take the document to King Eristan." The man handed him the parchment.

Eristan studied the peasant. "Sir, who gave you this parchment?"

"I—I do not know, sire. The man was a total stranger. He approached me just outside the gates of Barrington Castle and offered me a five-klorin piece if I would bring the parchment to you. Five klorins is a lot of money, Your Majesty, and so I agreed. That's all I know."

Eristan beckoned to the sentry. "Take this man to the other end of the great hall and feed him if necessary, but keep him here for the next hour or so, should we have further questions."

"Aye, sire." The sentry led the man away.

Eristan looked at Sir Reginald. "Pa, why don't you read the document to us?"

"As you wish, Your Majesty." Reginald unrolled the parchment and glanced at it. "It's signed by Vladimir, sire, and at first glance the signature appears to be genuine."

"Read it aloud."

Sir Reginald cleared his throat and read aloud the following message:

*"Young Eristan
Barrington Castle*

To the would-be king and his would-be court. The throne of Cheswold is rightly mine, though I did not oppose you on your coronation day. I now hold something of great value to you, and I am willing to negotiate. I will contact you within a fortnight.

*Regards,
King Vladimir"*

"Of all the arrogance!" Lord Wallace fumed. "He writes as if he were the rightful king of Cheswold!"

"This removes all doubt that Vladimir is responsible for Princess Cordelia's abduction," Melzar commented. "He plans to trade her life for the throne."

"That despicable monster," Eristan growled. "If he touches one hair on her head . . ."

"He won't harm her, sire," Lord Wallace assured him. "She's

too valuable to him, sire, but only if she is alive and well. He and his men won't dare touch her, for her value to them lies in the fact that he plans to use her to negotiate."

"Call the peasant before me again," Eristan ordered.

Moments later the peasant knelt once again before the king. "Sir, describe the man who gave you the parchment."

"He was a knight of Cheswold, sire, and riding a roan warhorse. He was wearing a chain mail hauberk and a battle helmet. That's all I know."

"Would you recognize him if you saw him again?"

"I doubt it, sire. As I said, he was wearing a helmet."

"Did he say anything about a return reply?"

"Nay, sire. After he handed me the parchment and the silver piece, he rode away from the castle in great haste. He didn't wait for a reply, sire."

"You may go," Eristan told the peasant, "but do not discuss this matter with anyone. Not one word—is that understood?"

The peasant nodded agreeably. "Aye, Your Majesty. Not one word, sire."

"Do not even mention this to your wife or family," King Eristan said sternly. "This is a matter of national security and you are to discuss this with no one. Do you understand me?"

The man bowed low. "Aye, sire. My lips are sealed. I will not breathe a word to anyone, sire."

"What is your name, sir?" Lord Wallace asked. "Where are you from?"

"I am Peyton of Gann, sire. I am a coppersmith by trade."

"You may go, Peyton of Gann," young King Eristan told the peasant. "See that you are mindful of my instructions. Not one word of this matter to anyone." The sentry escorted the man from the great hall.

Later that evening, under a moon that was nearly full, King Eristan and Sir Reginald walked on the balcony belonging to Eristan's chambers. A cool mist hung in the air, creating a shimmering halo around the moon. "I fear for Cordelia's life, Pa," the young king confessed, and his voice trembled. "Lord Wallace assures me that Vladimir won't harm her, but how do we know that? He'll stop at nothing to regain the throne. Cordelia's life means nothing to him."

"His purpose in holding her is to force you to abdicate the throne to him," Reginald reminded him. "Lord Wallace is right—Vladimir will not harm her, for that would not serve his purpose."

"And so you think he will demand that I surrender the throne in exchange for her return?"

Reginald nodded. "That would seem to be his plan."

The young king trembled with emotion. "What am I to do, Pa? I cannot surrender the throne, for all Cheswold is counting on me. I intend to secure our borders and rebuild our armies in order to defend Cheswold against Karnivan invasions, but I know that Vladimir will not do that. Pa, I cannot surrender the throne to him.

"And yet, Vladimir holds Cordelia captive. I cannot refuse his demands, knowing that I might forfeit my sister's life if I do. Pa, what course of action am I to take?"

"Your first course of action should be to send a petition to King Emmanuel," Sir Reginald reminded gently. "He knows where Cordelia is, Son. If you look to him, Emmanuel can guide you and your men in your quest to rescue her. He alone can keep her safe."

"Aye, Pa," the young king replied quietly. "Let's do it now."

Moments later, two petitions streaked across the darkened skies on their way to the throne room of the Golden City of the Redeemed.

"I will send petitions many times in the next few days," Sir Reginald promised, "and you must do the same. Seek Emmanuel's guidance as we prepare to rescue Cordelia, and seek his guidance as you fortify Cheswold against the Karnivans." He looked up at the velvet sky and shivered. "Let's head inside, shall we? I'm about to freeze out here."

As they walked back inside, Eristan remembered the mysterious parchment with the invisible writing. "Pa, come into my chambers," he invited. "I want you to see something."

A moment later Sir Reginald stood in the doorway of the royal bedchamber, his eyes dancing as he admired the elegant setting and the luxurious appointments. "Quite a change from a carpenter's hut, isn't it?" he teased. "Dathan, my son, you've come a long way."

"You called me Dathan."

Reginald grinned. "Just wanted to remind you that you once lived as the poorest of peasants. Don't take the finery and the luxury for granted."

"Look at this, Pa," Eristan said, opening the drawer of the chiffonier and withdrawing the enigmatic parchment. "What do you make of it?"

Reginald read the cryptic message aloud.

> *"In a city forbidden,*
> *Doth the lion crouch deep.*
> *A treasure lies hidden*
> *Though far from the keep."*

He frowned when he finished. "Where did you get this?" Turning the parchment over, he studied the strange diagram on the back. "This looks like some sort of a map. Eristan, where did this come from?"

"A peasant gave it to Sterling with instructions to give it to me," the young king replied. "Sterling and I think that the map is actually a diagram of a castle."

Reginald considered the diagram for a long moment. "You may very well be right."

"Pa, what is the meaning of the message? 'In a city forbidden doth the lion crouch deep.' What in Terrestria does that mean?"

Reginald frowned. "Your father was known as the 'Lion of Cheswold.' He was a brilliant battle tactician and when he went to war, he and his men fought like lions. Perhaps this is a reference to him."

"Why does it say that the lion crouches deep? That's a peculiar choice of words."

Sir Reginald shrugged. "Perhaps it refers to his burial."

King Eristan studied the parchment. "In a city forbidden," he read aloud. "Pa, where would that be?"

Sir Reginald shrugged. "Xanterra, perhaps."

"Zan—what?"

"Xanterra," Reginald replied. "The Forbidden City."

"What's the Forbidden City?" Eristan asked. "I've never heard of it."

"Xanterra was a tiny city built in a mountain pass in southwestern Cheswold," Reginald replied, "right on the border between Cheswold and Karniva. Many years ago, King William learned that many of the people of Xanterra were Karnivan sympathizers and were helping Karnivan raiders enter the country, even housing and feeding them. The king sent a garrison of soldiers to destroy the city and forced the inhabitants to relocate in other parts of Cheswold. He left a small garrison of knights in Xanterra Castle to guard the pass and decreed that the city would never be rebuilt; thus it became known as the Forbidden City."

Eristan stared at the words on the parchment. "So my father is buried in the Forbidden City?"

Sir Reginald shook his head. "I doubt that."

"Just what is left of Xanterra now?" Eristan asked, as Captain Orwyn approached.

"Not much," the captain replied, entering the conversation. "Nine or ten years ago a powerful earthquake struck the city and an enormous rockslide destroyed the castle, burying much of it, and forever closing off the pass. Several of the knights were killed and Vladimir brought the remaining ones home to Barrington."

"So no one lives there now?"

"Mountain goats and scavenger birds, perhaps," the captain answered. "It's a barren, desolate place that no one would ever want to visit."

"A city forbidden," the young king repeated, looking at the parchment. "Would that refer to Xanterra?"

"I doubt it," Sir Reginald replied. "True, Xanterra is called the Forbidden City, but there's nothing there now. As Captain Orwyn said, the garrison of knights was called back to Barrington Castle when the pass was closed by the rockslide."

"Have you ever been there?" Eristan inquired of both men.

Sir Reginald shook his head, but Captain Orwyn hesitated. "Aye," he said finally, "I have. It was I who led the brigade of knights that destroyed the city."

Eristan was stunned. "What happened to the people?"

"We harmed no one," Captain Orwyn said quickly. "We forced the inhabitants to evacuate and then destroyed most of the buildings. We left the castle intact, of course, as well as a few other buildings. Everything was later destroyed in the earthquake and the rockslide."

"I'd like to see Xanterra," Eristan mused. "The story is fascinating."

"It's not a place that you would care to visit," Reginald insisted. "It's a treacherous, desolate place that was once home to a band of Cheswoldians who were disloyal to your father. Xanterra reeks of treachery and death."

The young king laughed. "It can't be that bad." He glanced once more at the mysterious document and then re-rolled it. "I'd give anything to learn what this message means. And I'd give a hundred klorins to find out who sent it to me."

He moved to replace the parchment in the drawer and then gave a startled exclamation.

"What is it?" Reginald asked.

"The golden dagger!" Eristan replied, staring at the empty chiffonier drawer. "It was right here under the map, but now it's gone!"

Chapter Thirteen

Sir Reginald, Captain Orwyn, and King Eristan stared at each other for a long moment and then turned as one to search the drawer of the chiffonier. "It's gone!" Eristan repeated, frantically pulling out other drawers. "The golden dagger is gone! It was right here in the top drawer, but now it's gone."

"Did anyone else know that the dagger was hidden here?" Sir Reginald asked.

Eristan turned to face him. "Oh, Pa," he groaned. "The only ones who knew were Cordelia and Sterling. We both know that Cordelia didn't take it, so . . ."

Sir Reginald frowned. "So you think Sterling took it."

"There's no proof as yet, Pa," Eristan replied impatiently, "but it does look mighty suspicious, doesn't it? My sister was abducted by a band of disloyal Cheswoldian knights, and Sterling was seen riding with them. He was one of the few people who knew that Tranquility was Cordelia's hideaway, and he could very well have been the one who led Vladimir's men to her. Now the golden dagger disappears, and Sterling and Cordelia are the only ones who knew it was in the drawer. We both know that Cordelia didn't steal it, so where does that leave us?"

"I can't imagine for one moment that Sterling would steal

the dagger," Sir Reginald retorted angrily, "and I know that he would not have helped Vladimir's men capture Cordelia. You saved his life at Windstone—do you honestly think that he would repay you by abducting your sister and stealing the dagger? Son, you do your friend an injustice by questioning his loyalty. Sterling is as loyal to the crown as I am."

Captain Orwyn spoke up. "Sir Reginald is right, sire. Sterling would not have stolen the dagger."

"The evidence seems to point to him," Eristan replied evenly. "What am I supposed to think?"

"We don't have much evidence as yet," Sir Reginald said. "Perhaps we need to gather more information before we jump to conclusions. Personally, I think you need to have a little more faith in your friend's loyalty until hard evidence proves otherwise."

Eristan sighed heavily. "Pa, don't you think that I want to believe in Sterling's loyalty? I hope more than anything that he was not the one to betray Cordelia and that he was not the one who stole the dagger, but the evidence seems to indicate otherwise."

"Circumstantial, at best."

Eristan nodded. "True enough. And as I said, I hope I'm wrong. I hope Sterling is innocent."

Sir Reginald yawned. "Son, let's get some sleep. It's been a long day."

King Eristan was just sitting down to breakfast when he saw Lord Wallace enter the great hall, so he summoned a servant. "Tell Lord Wallace that I would like for him to have breakfast at my table."

The servant bowed low. "Aye, sire."

Moments later the chief magistrate approached the king's table. "Good morning, Your Majesty."

"Lord Wallace, dine with me. I'd like to ask you some questions as we eat."

"Certainly, sire."

Eristan waited until the magistrate had been served and then asked, "Sir, do you remember the events surrounding my father's death? Do you know where he was buried?"

Lord Wallace looked up from his toast. "Fourteen long years have passed since the night when Barrington Castle was besieged and King William was killed," he replied quietly. "Memories fade with the passage of time, sire."

"But you were there," the young king persisted. "What can you tell me about my father's death?"

"There is much that I do not know about your father's death," the magistrate said slowly, "but I do know that the Karnivans invaded Cheswold, besieged Barrington Castle, and eventually took the castle. King William was killed on the night the castle was taken, but not before he somehow had you and your sister spirited away to safety. Three days later, Captain Furlton rallied the troops and retook the castle, and eventually, drove the Karnivans from Cheswold."

"And for the past fourteen years Cheswold has lived under the constant threat of invasion by Grimlor and the Karnivans," Eristan finished.

"Exactly," Lord Wallace agreed. "If your father had lived, I'm sure the Karnivans would have been subdued long ago. He was a powerful warrior and brilliant in battle strategy, and Cheswold's army was strong. His men loved him and would have followed him into the very jaws of death. Vladimir, however, was weak and vacillating and allowed the army to deteriorate. He even disbanded the cavalry units, though Cheswold needed them desperately."

"Why did Vladimir disband Cheswold's cavalry?"

The magistrate shrugged. "I do not know. At any rate, Garven stood up to him publicly—he was commander of the cavalry units, you know—and Vladimir was furious. He relieved him of his command and even considered executing him, I'm afraid. Lord Keidric quickly gave him a position as stablemaster at Windstone Castle just to get him out of Vladimir's sight, and Vladimir promptly forgot the matter."

"So if my father had lived, Cheswold could very well be at peace right now."

Lord Wallace nodded. "That's a very real possibility."

Three days later, King Eristan and Sir Reginald stood on the sentry walk above the main gate of Barrington Castle. Eristan leaned his elbows on the nearest merlon and leaned over, looking at the drawbridge below. "Give me an update on the castle defenses, Pa. As constable, you know better than anyone what condition the garrisons are in. What can I expect to find?"

"We're making excellent progress," Reginald reported, "but we do have a long way to go. As you know, Vladimir had allowed discipline to become lax, and training was a thing of the past. Morale among the troops was pathetic. But with the daily training exercises under Melzar, the men's battle skills are improving rapidly. I am working with both garrisons in the evenings, training the troops in specific skills in regards to the defense of Barrington Castle. The garrisons are making excellent progress, sire."

"With you and Melzar working with the troops, I'm sure they are, Pa."

"What progress are we making with the border defenses?" Sir Reginald asked.

"Captain Orwyn and his men are working on it night and day," the young king replied, "but we have a long way to go before we can consider the borders secure. Cheswold is still vulnerable to invasion by the Karnivans, Pa, and that worries me."

"Send regular petitions to King Emmanuel," Reginald replied. "You know what the King's book says: 'Except Emmanuel build the house, they labor in vain that build it: except Emmanuel keep the city, the watchman waketh but in vain.' We must do what we can to fortify our defenses, but security and safety must come from His Majesty."

Eristan nodded. "I know, Pa, and we do send regular petitions." He glanced down at the castle approach. "Who are those men?"

As the king and the constable watched, a dozen peasant farmers toiled up the steep castle approach. When they neared the drawbridge they were stopped by a sentry, who talked with them for several minutes. At last, the sentry entered the castle and hurried up the stairs to the sentry walk.

"Your Majesty, a group of peasants from one of the border villages are requesting an audience with you. Sire, their village was burned last night by mounted raiders."

"Another border village burned." King Eristan sighed. "This is the second one this week." He studied the peasants for a moment. "Bring them to me."

"Sire, do you want additional bodyguards? Would you prefer to see the visitors in the great hall?"

The young king shook his head. "They look distressed and

weary from their journey. I will see them at once here in the bailey so that they may tell their story. Afterwards, take them to the great hall and feed them. Do what you can to encourage them."

"Aye, sire, I will show them in immediately." The sentry hurried down the stairs.

Moments later, the peasants crossed the bailey hesitantly, fearfully, and then fell on their faces some ten paces from King Eristan and Sir Reginald. "Rise, my good men," Eristan urged, striding toward the prostrate group. "The sentry tells me that you have suffered a great loss and that you have traveled far. Please, tell me your story."

Hesitantly, the men stood. The tallest of the group stepped forward, bowing repeatedly. "My lord, last night our village was burned by raiders. Everything was destroyed, sire, and we have nowhere to go."

"What is your name, sir?"

"Lawrence, my lord." The man bowed again. "I am the village reeve."

"Lawrence, was anyone killed in the attack?"

"Nay, sire, no one was even hurt, but every one of our homes was destroyed. There's nothing left, my lord. We have nowhere to go."

"Was it Karnivan raiders?"

"We believe it was, Your Majesty, but we're not certain." Lawrence's voice rose in pitch. "They said that we crossed the border, sire, and killed three of their people, and that the raid on our village was retaliation for the attack. We didn't cross the border, sire. We don't dare cross the border."

Eristan nodded. "They seek to intimidate us. Grimlor wants Cheswold, and he'll stop at nothing to get it." He smiled reassuringly at the weary men. "Follow the sentry to the great hall to get some food and drink. We will talk again later when you have had some refreshment and some rest."

"We are grateful, Your Majesty." The peasants bowed low as Eristan and Reginald again climbed the stairs to the sentry walk.

"Karnivan raids on border villages are becoming more and more frequent, Pa, but what I really worry about is a full-scale invasion. Our border is still vulnerable and Grimlor is taking advantage of that, but what if he decides to invade? Border security must be our top priority, and we must move fast."

"And we still have Vladimir to contend with," Sir Reginald growled, "though we have heard nothing from him."

"The trackers lost the trail of Cordelia's abductors when they passed though the city of Abingdon," King Eristan said. "So now we have no leads to follow. Pa, what are we going to do to get Cordelia back safely if we don't even know where she is?"

"Emmanuel knows," Sir Reginald replied quietly. "He can guide us to her. Vladimir will contact you again when he is ready to make his demands. Perhaps we can have spies track his men back to her."

The young king shook his head. "Vladimir is too clever for that, Pa. You and I both know that he would never allow that to happen."

Reginald sighed. "I'm afraid you're right. It was just a wistful thought." He looked thoughtful for a moment and then turned to Eristan. "Do you know who could do it, if anybody could? Your friend Sterling."

"Sterling?" Eristan snorted. "Sterling is just a youth."

"Aye, but so are you," Reginald retorted, "yet you sit upon the throne of Cheswold as our king. And a fine one you will be, too, once you determine to serve your people rather than your own selfish desires."

"But Sterling is so young," Eristan replied, ignoring the remark about his own rule. "I just can't imagine him effective as an agent for Cheswold."

"Lord Stephen tells me that Sterling has served on multiple assignments," Sir Reginald told him. "According to him, Sterling is one of the best agents that Cheswold has ever had. He's quick-witted and clever, and he doesn't panic when he gets into a tight situation. And because he is so young, folks seem to trust him."

"I trusted him," the young king said bitterly, "and it's beginning to look as if he betrayed me."

"We don't know that," Reginald replied quickly. "Wait until you have the opportunity to hear his side of it."

"He was riding with Cordelia's abductors," Eristan snarled. "What more proof do we need?"

"Perchance there is more to this than we can see."

Eristan was exasperated. "Pa, what more do we need to know? The golden dagger is missing—only Sterling and Cordelia knew where it was. Then Cordelia was abducted by a band of men and Sterling was seen riding among them. Apparently he was the one who led them to her." He set his jaw. "Tomorrow I will issue a decree for Sterling's arrest. I want him hunted down and brought to stand trial before me. Pa, unless he can prove his innocence, I will have him hanged as a traitor to Cheswold."

Chapter Fourteen

Five days passed with no message from Vladimir and no word as to Cordelia's whereabouts. King Eristan suspended one entire battalion from battle training and sent them on a full scale manhunt for Sterling with orders to bring him back alive, if possible, but to take any measures necessary to accomplish his capture. Sir Reginald and Melzar both tried their best to persuade him not to issue the edict, but their words fell on deaf ears. In his desperation to find his twin sister, the young king had become irrational.

"I want to trust Sterling, Pa, but the evidence is against him," Eristan replied one evening during dinner in the great hall as Sir Reginald attempted to reason with him. "When he stands trial he'll have the opportunity to speak for himself. But unless he has hard evidence to verify his story, he'll hang as a traitor."

"You've already made up your mind as to his guilt," the nobleman retorted. "What chance does he have of proving anything if his end has already been determined?"

"He'll stand before the High Council for judgment, not before me," the young king snapped, "though I certainly plan to be present."

"Perchance the High Council will exhibit less bias than my

king does," Reginald growled softly. "Were Sterling to stand before you, his guilt would already be established."

"Do you question my judgment, Pa?"

"Nay, I simply wish that you would show a little more faith in your friend."

At that moment there was a slight disturbance at the door of the great hall and they both looked up to see a group of men gathered around a knight who had just entered. The men were discussing something in animated tones. "He bears tidings, Son," Sir Reginald observed. "Perhaps he has word of Cordelia, or of Sterling."

A knight approached the table and bowed to Eristan. "Begging your pardon for interrupting your dinner, sire, but I knew you would want to know as soon as possible. The traitor Sterling has been captured, sire. He is being taken to the dungeon even as we speak."

Eristan felt a wave of emotion sweep over him. "Take the wretch to the chambers of the High Council immediately," he directed, "and order the Council to assemble at once. This is the moment for which we have waited."

Within minutes the High Council had been assembled. As the magistrates took their places, King Eristan found a seat to one side. At his request, Sir Reginald and the other members of the cabinet were also present. Eristan addressed the guard. "We're all here. Bring in the traitor that he might stand trial for his crimes against Cheswold."

"Aye, Your Majesty."

The door opened and Sterling was ushered into the room with his hands bound tightly behind him and shackles upon his feet. A look of bewilderment swept across his handsome features as he approached Eristan. "Eristan, this has been a big mistake. Your men have arrested—"

"Silence!" Eristan roared. "Traitor, you'll speak only when you are given permission to do so."

Stunned, Sterling stopped in mid-sentence. His eyes widened in astonishment and a look of dismay swept across his features as he bowed his head. "Aye, Your Majesty. I beg pardon, sire." Abruptly he lifted his head and looked King Eristan in the eye. "Eristan, please hear me out. I know where Cordelia is."

"I'm sure you do, wretch, for you played a part in her capture."

"I assure you that I had no part in her capture, my king, but I followed her captors and I know where she was taken. She's being held in the dungeon at Trandor Castle—"

"I would advise you to say no more," Eristan snapped. He struggled to keep his voice from trembling as he growled, "You, sir, are charged with high treason against the kingdom of Cheswold and numerous crimes against the crown. In particular, you are charged with conspiracy to abduct Princess Cordelia and with actually taking part in the deed. Furthermore, you are charged with the theft of the golden dagger belonging to the crown jewels of the throne of Cheswold. I will not hear your case and you will make no defense to me. Lord Wallace and the High Council will hear your case and to them you will make your defense, if indeed you have one."

Rage flooded his soul, and he paused in an attempt to control his emotions. "Sterling, you are despicable. I had thought you my friend, yet you have betrayed me and my country and jeopardized the life of my sister. It's a fine way to repay me for the kindnesses I have shown you."

Sterling bowed his head.

The young king turned to Lord Wallace. "Sir, you and the High Council are to conduct the questioning and investigation of the matter."

Lord Wallace nodded soberly. "Aye, Your Majesty." Addressing Sterling, he said, "Prisoner, approach the bench." Slowly, soberly, Sterling approached the Council and stood before them with head held high as he deliberately made eye contact with each magistrate. Eristan was amazed at his boldness. Lord Wallace cleared his throat. "State your name."

"I am Sterling of Marden. My father is Lord Stephen, Duke of Marden. I am a loyal son of Cheswold."

Eristan glanced at Lord Stephen and saw that the duke was rigid. His eyes gave evidence of his anxiety.

"Sterling of Marden, you stated that you know the whereabouts of Princess Cordelia. Is this true?"

"Aye, sire, that is correct."

"Sir, how do you come by such information? Our best men have searched for the princess, but with no success."

"Sire, I witnessed the abduction of the princess. I followed Vladimir's men when they took her."

"You *rode with* Vladimir's men," King Eristan interrupted, with a snarl. "You took part in her capture. A witness identified you."

Sterling shook his head vehemently. "Please do not think that of me, Your Majesty. Why would I participate in the capture of Princess Cordelia? She is my friend, just as you are."

Eristan snorted. "Bite your tongue, rogue. You are no friend of mine."

"Your Majesty, I remain your friend, though at present you seem to disbelieve me."

"Sir," Lord Wallace said, "a witness saw you riding with Vladimir's men and apparently participating in the capture of the princess. How do you explain your presence in the glen, and how do you explain the fact that you were seen riding with the company of knights that abducted the princess?"

Sterling took a deep breath and let it out slowly. "The glen was one of Cordelia's favorite places to find solitude. She called it 'Tranquility' and she loved to go there to be alone. On the day in question, I knew that Princess Cordelia was planning to visit the glen. I went to the glen ahead of her, intending to surprise her as a joke. As I entered the glen I saw signs that a number of horses had recently entered the glen, and I also saw that efforts had been made to erase the tracks. At once I knew that something sinister was afoot.

"As I turned to run back to Barrington Castle to warn Princess Cordelia, a sentry accosted me, holding me at sword point as he intended to take me to the rest of the company. At that moment I saw Princess Cordelia and Lady Marta enter the glen, though they were some hundred yards from me, and I knew that it was forever too late to warn the princess. I did the first thing that came to mind—I knocked the sentry unconscious, took his hauberk and helmet and put them on, and then found his horse and appropriated it for myself.

"It was at that moment that the princess was seized and thrown across a horse, while Lady Marta was thrown rudely to the ground. Deciding to follow Vladimir's men, I rode after them and joined their company, but not before I had revealed myself to Lady Marta in hopes that she would notify His Majesty that I was among Vladimir's men. I had hoped that the news would bring hope to your heart, my king."

Sterling sighed. "I rode with the abductors all the way to Trandor Castle, where Princess Cordelia was immediately imprisoned in the castle dungeon."

"Why did you not return immediately to Barrington Castle to sound the alarm instead of riding off with Vladimir's men?" Lord Wallace asked sharply.

"I—I only had a brief instant to make a decision, sire. I

was sure that Lady Marta would run to the castle and sound the alarm, and so I figured it would be better for me to try to ride with Vladimir's men in order to find out where the princess was being taken."

"Vladimir's men did not discover your identity?"

"Nay, sire, apparently not. I accompanied them all the way to Trandor Castle, yet my presence was not noticed."

"If you are not one of them, sir, you would have been killed immediately, had you been discovered. Were you not aware of that?"

Sterling nodded. "Aye, sire, I was aware."

"And yet you took that chance?"

Sterling let out his breath slowly. "Since I was wearing the helmet and hauberk of one of Vladimir's men, I had hopes that my identity would not be discovered. I knew that I would forfeit my life if I was discovered, yet I was willing to take that chance. If I could learn the location where the princess would be held hostage, perhaps a rescue could be planned."

Lord Wallace spoke again. "Your story sounds good, sir, but I have a problem with it. Captain Vance tells me that his men captured you some distance north of Trandor Castle. Barrington Castle lies southeast of Trandor. If you knew the location of Princess Cordelia, why did you not return to Barrington with the news in order to affect a rescue attempt?"

"In talking with the guards at Trandor Castle, I heard tales of an old hermit who supposedly could appear and disappear at will, often apparating himself into the castle dungeon. They call him 'the Phantom of Trandor.' I suspect that the man simply knew of a secret passage into the dungeon and that the tales of his unusual powers grew from the fact that he could come and go at will. I am told that the Phantom lives in the

Forest of Trandor. I was attempting to find him when I was arrested by Captain Vance and his men."

A stern look appeared on the face of the chief magistrate. "And what were your intentions, sir?"

"I had hoped to find the Phantom and determine if there really is a secret passage into the castle, sire. I then intended to return to Barrington Castle with the news and help organize an assault force to make a rescue attempt."

"Why should we believe your story? What proof do you have?" Eristan glanced at the High Council and saw that the magistrates seemed unconvinced.

"I have no proof, sire. Perhaps if we can find the Phantom of Trandor that would help corroborate my story, but other than that, I have no proof."

"What happened to the golden dagger?" King Eristan demanded. "You and Cordelia were the only ones who knew where it was hidden, and we both know that she did not take it."

Sterling shrugged his shoulders in a bewildered sort of way. "I have no idea, Your Majesty, I really do not. I only know that I had nothing to do with its disappearance."

Lord Wallace and the other magistrates began to question Sterling about the golden dagger, and as they did, Eristan sat silently, carefully watching Sterling for any facial expression that would betray his words. But his answers were forthright and clear, without hesitation, and his countenance seemed to radiate sincerity. *What if he is telling the truth?* the young king asked himself in dismay. *He seems sincere and his words ring of truth. If he is telling the truth, I am the biggest fool in Cheswold! Oh, Sterling, how could I have doubted you?*

Eristan gestured for Sir Reginald and Lord Wallace to approach. "What do you think?" he asked in a low voice, as the men leaned close. "Is Sterling telling the truth?"

"He seems to be," Sir Reginald replied, "though there is no way to know for sure. His story makes sense, and it certainly would be consistent with the Sterling that I know."

Eristan looked at Lord Wallace. "What do you think, sir?"

"His story is convincing," the chief Magistrate replied. "If he's not telling the truth, he's the smoothest liar I have ever encountered."

"Should we believe him?"

"We have no reason to disbelieve him," Sir Reginald said. "His story rings of truth, and as I said, it seems consistent with his character."

"What about the disappearance of the golden dagger? He has not explained that."

"Perhaps he is telling the truth and knows nothing about it."

"Oh, Pa," King Eristan said with remorse, "if Sterling is telling the truth, I have made the biggest mistake of my life! If he really did risk his life by riding with Vladimir's men in order to locate Cordelia, what a fool I have been to reward him by arresting him and calling him a liar! If he is telling the truth, he is one of the best friends I have, yet I have treated him as an enemy."

"If he is truly a friend he will find it in his heart to forgive you," Sir Reginald replied quietly.

"And if he is not telling the truth he deserves to hang," Eristan said, as an intense feeling of dread swept over him. "How are we to know?"

Chapter Fifteen

Silence ruled in the chambers of the High Council of Cheswold as Sterling stood before King Eristan. Sterling took a deep breath and then hesitantly approached the king, dropping to one knee five paces from him. "The Forest of Trandor is two days' ride from here, my lord," he said quietly, though everyone in the chambers of the High Council could hear him. "Please allow me to take one battalion and search for the Phantom."

He swallowed hard and then continued. "If there is indeed a secret passage into the dungeons and we can locate it, we will have the element of surprise. Far better it would be to slip into the castle undetected than to attempt to battle our way in. If we can slip into the dungeons through a subterranean passage without encountering Vladimir's men, our chances of success are much greater and the risks to Cordelia would be—"

As Sterling said Cordelia's name his voice broke and his eyes welled with tears. King Eristan looked at him in surprise. "Sterling?"

"Aye, my lord?"

"Are you all right?"

"Aye, my lord." Sterling's voice was husky with emotion.

Eristan felt as if a cold knife had just been driven into his heart, and his mouth suddenly became dry. His voice trembled as he said, "You really do care about her, don't you? Oh, Sterling, how could I ever have been so wrong?"

"Cordelia's life is in peril, my lord. We must make haste."

The young king leaped from the chair and engulfed his friend in an embrace. "You must find it in your heart to forgive me, my friend. Oh, Sterling, how could I have been so wrong?"

Sterling returned the hug. "Eristan, you and Cordelia are the best friends I have. How could I have plotted against you?"

Eristan's eyes stung. "I see that now. Forgive me, please forgive me, for doubting you."

"All is forgiven and forgotten, Your Majesty. We must get on with the matter of rescuing your sister."

The young king took a deep breath and raised his voice. "My friend Sterling is innocent and is cleared of all charges. This case is dismissed and will never be referred to again. And now we must make plans for a rescue operation. Tonight we ride for the Forest of Trandor."

Four hours later, sixty mounted knights rode from Barrington Castle under the cover of darkness, King Eristan, Sir Reginald, and Sterling among them. Slipping from the castle in groups of six or eight to avoid attracting attention, they assembled in a moonlit meadow two miles west of the castle. "I still say that you should remain in the safety of Barrington Castle," Sir Reginald told Eristan, as they sat their horses and waited for the remainder of the task force to arrive. "As the king of Cheswold, you must not take chances with your life. This mission could prove to be quite dangerous."

"Cordelia is my sister," the young king answered resolutely, "and I will be present when she is rescued. Let's have no more talk about my safety."

Reginald shrugged. "As you wish, sire."

When the strike force was assembled, King Eristan stood in the stirrups and raised his voice. "Tonight we ride on a mission of the utmost importance. The life of the princess hangs in the balance, and it is up to us to see that she makes it safely home to Barrington Castle. As your king, I wish to express my gratitude to each of you for volunteering for this perilous mission. Let's ride."

Long purple shadows were stealing across the moors as Sterling reined his stallion in beside King Eristan. At his signal, the company of mounted knights came to a halt. "It's been a hard two days of riding," Sterling said, "but Trandor Castle lies less than ten miles to the west, sire, just beyond that series of rolling hills." He stood in the stirrups and pointed. "If we ride up this valley and then follow the river westward a few miles, it will bring us to the forest where we hope to find the Phantom." He gave a wry grin. "That's where your men arrested me."

Eristan gave him an apologetic look. "I'm sorry it happened that way."

Sterling nodded soberly. "You should be sorry. If your men hadn't delayed me, I would probably have been back at Barrington Castle two days ago with the information that we are seeking." Abruptly, he laughed to show Eristan that he was jesting. "What's done is done. With Emmanuel's guidance, perhaps we can make up for lost time."

Eristan paused. "Sterling, are you certain, dead certain, that my sister is in the dungeon at Trandor Castle?"

Sterling nodded. "I saw her with my own eyes. She's in a double security cell on the west side of the dungeon."

"But you actually saw her?"

"Aye, my lord. She is guarded day and night by two guards: one of Vladimir's men and one from the Trandor garrison. On the second night I managed to get myself placed on the third watch so that I could see her for myself. I felt that it was necessary to ascertain that she is actually in the Trandor dungeon. I had hoped to get a message of encouragement to her, but with the other guard present, the opportunity never presented itself."

"Did you speak to her?" Eristan asked eagerly.

"Nay, my lord, but she did see me and recognize me. When the other guard was not looking for a moment, I made signs to let her know that we are making plans to free her. I think she understood."

The young king let out his breath in a long sigh. "I thank you, Sterling, for you have given me hope."

Sir Reginald had been listening to this interchange and now he rode forward. "Describe the dungeon," he requested. "What are our chances for a successful rescue?"

"Not good unless there is a secret passage," Sterling replied. "There are four men posted day and night outside the main entrance and two more inside each cell block. There is no way we could fight our way in without raising a general alarm. Unless there is indeed a secret passage and a way to slip into the cell blocks undetected, we don't have a chance."

"So our only hope is to find the Phantom."

Sterling nodded. "So it would seem, sire."

"Let us hope that he is more than just a legend."

Sterling turned his horse. "Let's ride. We have barely an hour of daylight left."

After a hard ride of several miles the riders left the river and rode into the forest just as darkness swept across the land like a cascade of black ink. King Eristan reined the stallion to a halt. "We can't travel like this," he observed. "It's so dark I can't see my horse's ears. We'll have to make camp for the night."

"Sire," one of the knights called, riding back toward King Eristan, "there's a cabin just ahead. Perhaps we can ask for directions there."

"Have the men prepare a campsite right here," Eristan told Sir Reginald. "Sterling and I will make a visit to the cabin. Perhaps we can pick up some information."

"Take a few men with you, please, Your Majesty," the nobleman suggested. "We don't know who or what you will encounter."

The young king nodded. "Aye. Send four knights with me."

As Eristan and Sterling approached the cottage, the four knights hovered a few paces behind them. "Take caution, Your Majesty," one warned in a low voice. "You don't want to walk into an ambush, sire."

"The place does look rather sinister, doesn't it?" Eristan remarked, leaning close to Sterling as he spoke. "Whoever built it didn't place it here to attract visitors. One would hardly notice it in broad daylight."

The cabin seemed to flow from the side of the ridge as if it were part of the mountain itself. The carefully chinked log walls were shrouded in tangles of ivy and the shake roof was dark with moss. The tiny structure gave the impression that it had sprung from the earth rather than being constructed by human hands.

"I don't know how your men ever spotted it," Sterling agreed. "Come on; let's see if anyone is at home."

"Stay where you are or your leader gets a bolt through the heart!" a rough voice shouted, and a blaze of yellow light streaked across the darkness. Eristan's heart pounded madly as the light rose high in the air and then hurtled back at him. Leaping clear of the blazing light, he realized that it was nothing more than a lantern swinging at the end of a chain. The four knights drew their swords and bounded forward.

"Sheath your weapons at once or your leader dies!" the unseen voice snarled. "He doesn't get a second chance!"

"Do what he says," King Eristan ordered, and the knights complied.

"What business have you here?" the voice demanded.

Eristan glanced around but could see nothing but his own companions and the surrounding darkness. The lantern still swung to and fro, and he knew that their assailant could see them clearly. The inhabitant of the cabin was shrewd and had easily placed his visitors at a disadvantage.

"What business have you here?" the voice demanded again, impatient and threatening. "Answer me."

Nervously, Eristan cleared his throat. "We're looking for a man known as the Phantom," he replied, trying to keep his voice from trembling.

"The Phantom." The voice was sarcastic, almost jeering. "Surely you do not believe in phantoms, sir."

Eristan took a deep breath. The lantern was now revolving in a slow ellipse. "We have been told that the Phantom lives in these woods and that he can help us, sir. Perhaps you can tell us where we might find him?"

"Perhaps you can leave before I fill your carcass with steel," the voice replied. "I tell you, there is no phantom in these woods."

"We have been told of a man who lives in these woods who has the ability to slip in and out of the dungeon at Trandor Castle without being detected," King Eristan replied, doing his best to keep his temper in check, for the man's tone of voice was beginning to irritate him. "Do you or do you not know of such a man?"

"Tales of heroic deeds abound in Terrestria," the voice replied, "but only a fool believes every tale that comes to his ears."

Eristan felt his neck grow hot. "Sir, do you or do you not know of such a man?"

"If there were such a man and I knew where to find him, why should I share such information with the likes of you, sir?" the voice demanded.

"We have been told that a certain young girl is being held captive in Trandor Dungeon," Eristan replied, "and we need the Phantom's assistance in freeing her."

"On what basis should this girl be freed? Perhaps she does not deserve her freedom."

"I assure you, sir, she has done nothing worthy of imprisonment," the young king declared. "Vladimir is holding her in an attempt to seize the throne of Cheswold."

"Vladimir?" There was a note of incredulity in the voice. "Who is this girl?"

Eristan hesitated. "The prisoner of whom I speak is the Princess Cordelia, daughter of the late King William himself. As I said, Vladimir is holding her hostage in an attempt to wrest the throne from King Eristan."

"Then you must be King Eristan," the voice said in amazement as a tall, broad-shouldered man strode into the circle of light cast by the gently swaying lantern. In his hands he carried a loaded crossbow. "Forgive me, Your Majesty," the man said, bowing low. "I had no idea who you were, my lord. Please, excuse my impertinence and suspicions. With Karnivan sympathizers as numerous as they are, one cannot be too cautious."

The man bowed again. "I am Raul of Trandor, sire, at your service. I am the one they sometimes call 'the Phantom.' How may I be of service to my lord?"

"Is it true that you can come and go at will in Trandor Castle?"

"Aye, but there are limitations, of course, my lord," Raul replied. He stepped closer, and Eristan saw that he was slender of waist, with broad shoulders and large hands that suggested tremendous strength. He moved with the easy grace of a man who is at home in the woods. A short sword hung at his side.

"Can you take us into the dungeon?" Eristan asked.

"Aye, my lord, I can penetrate the dungeon," the tall woodsman replied, "but I would not take the group of you. It would be too dangerous."

"Could you help us find the princess?"

"Aye, if His Majesty desires that of me," Raul replied quietly, "but not only that, sire. I can rescue her, if that is as you wish."

Eristan was taken aback at the man's quiet confidence. "How would you do it, sir?"

The man hesitated. "What I am about to tell you I have told no man before, Your Majesty, and I tell you only because you are my king." He glanced at Sterling and the four knights and then looked back to Eristan. "My lord, may we talk in private?"

"Of course." Eristan gestured, and Sterling and the knights retreated into the darkness.

"My grandfather helped build Trandor Castle," Raul began. "He was a master stonemason and was in charge of most of the construction. Before he died he showed me a secret entrance that he had built. There is a passageway running along the main corridor of the dungeon and a secret panel at the bottom of the stairs that opens into the corridor. There are several peepholes in the secret passageway that allow one to see what is happening in the dungeon."

"But how could you rescue Cordelia?" the young king asked. "The dungeon is guarded day and night."

Raul grinned. "Time is wasting, sire. It would be far better to do the deed than to take the time to explain it to you, my lord."

Eristan nodded. "Aye. Then let us be off at once."

Raul hesitated. "You wish to go with me, sire?"

"Aye, Princess Cordelia is my sister."

"The danger is great, sire, and one man travels far more stealthily than two."

"Cordelia is my sister," the young king repeated. "I would be there when she is rescued, sir."

Raul shrugged. "As you wish, my lord. How soon can you be ready?"

"I am ready now."

The tall huntsman extended the crossbow to Eristan. "Has His Majesty had experience with the crossbow?"

"A little," Eristan replied, "though I am far more effective with the sword."

"Once we enter the dungeon, the crossbow will be of more service than the sword," Raul told him, handing him the weapon along with a small quiver of bolts. "If you will wait here, sire, I will return within the moment." With these words, the huntsman vanished into the darkness as if he were indeed a phantom, reappearing a moment later with a second crossbow strapped to his side. Eristan detected the smell of hot metal as Raul handed him a black object.

"A shadow lantern, my lord. I would ask that you not open the shutter except in an emergency. Our success depends upon the element of surprise. Without it, we are lost."

Eristan nodded. "Of course."

Sterling stepped close at that moment. "Asking permission to accompany you, my lord."

Eristan shook his head. "Raul says the fewer men we have, the better our chances of success. Make camp here and we'll meet back here. Do send a petition for us, though."

"That I will, Eristan."

"What cell was Cordelia in, Sterling?"

Sterling paused. "The last cell in the cell block to the west. You had to pass through two doors to reach it."

"Very well," Raul replied. "I know the very cell." He glanced at the velvet sky and then looked back to Eristan. "Ready, my lord? We must move quickly, my lord, but when we approach the castle we must move as silently as shadows. Stay within three paces of me and watch me at all times."

A thick bank of clouds glided in front of the moon, plunging the hillside into inky darkness as Raul and King Eristan made their way toward Trandor Castle. In spite of the darkness, the tall huntsman moved quickly and without hesitation as though he knew every step of the way, and Eristan struggled to keep up with him.

After crossing the ridge, traversing a broad, heath-covered moor, and skirting a brackish, foul-smelling swamp, Raul and Eristan made their way up a rugged slope. The huntsman halted when he reached the crest of the ridge. "Trandor Castle is less than two furlongs from us," he said in a hoarse whisper. "We must be completely silent as we descend the ridge. Stay close to me and take each step carefully."

Eristan's heart was in his throat as he followed Raul through the blackness of the night. Step by step, moving cautiously and as silently as phantoms, the huntsman and the young king approached the forbidding walls of Trandor Castle. Less than three hundred paces from the outer curtain wall, Raul dropped to his knees and crawled under a thicket. Eristan followed him.

Raul dropped his legs into a narrow cleft in the ground and then slowly disappeared from view as he slid his body into the dark opening. Eristan followed, his heart pounding with anticipation as he lowered himself into the waiting darkness. The huntsman opened the shutter on his dark lantern and Eristan could see that they were in a narrow underground corridor. "Use your lantern, but don't say a word," Raul told him. "Walk carefully and make as little noise as possible. Every sound we make is amplified a hundred times within the dungeon. We don't want the guards to hear us coming."

Eristan nodded. "Aye."

Traveling slowly and cautiously, the pair inched their way along the narrow corridor. As the corridor began to slope upward, Raul turned to Eristan. "We're now inside the castle," he whispered. "The dungeon is just ahead. Don't make a sound."

The corridor became so narrow that both men had to turn sideways as they inched their way along between the confining stone walls. At last, the tall huntsman halted and turned to Eristan, holding one finger to his lips. Reaching out, he closed the shutter on Eristan's lantern, concealing the light, and then closed his own lantern, plunging the corridor into darkness. Eristan's heart pounded.

Moments later Eristan became aware of a dim glow as Raul peered through a narrow fissure in the wall. As Eristan watched in silence, Raul took a hollow reed from within his jerkin, carefully placed a tiny object into the end of the reed, and then inserted the end of the tube in his mouth. Crouching slightly, he then put the opposite end into the fissure in the wall. Taking a deep breath, he blew abruptly and forcefully.

Eristan crouched slightly, peered into the fissure, and found that he was looking into the dungeon of Trandor Castle. A sputtering torch on the wall illuminated a row of narrow cells. A lone guard paced slowly down the dismal corridor. As Eristan watched, the guard abruptly stiffened and then fell headlong to the floor with a crash. Within seconds, a second guard rushed into the cellblock to investigate.

Seeing his fallen comrade, the guard drew his sword and hurried over. Bending over, he reached down and touched the fallen guard. At that moment, Eristan heard Raul blow forcefully on the reed a second time. The guard flinched, straightened up stiffly, and then seconds later fell unconscious to the floor.

"Let's go!" Raul urged. Opening the shutter on his lantern, he rushed to the end of the corridor. Pulling back a large iron bolt, he knelt and put his shoulder to the wall, pushing with all his might. To Eristan's amazement, the bottom of the wall slid away, revealing an opening. Raul dropped to his belly and wriggled through, calling "Follow me." Eristan complied without hesitation.

"Draw your sword, sire," Raul called as the young king stood to his feet inside the dungeon corridor.

Raul dashed to the cell at the far end of the cell block, peered inside for an instant, and then turned to the occupant of the next cell, a thin peasant. "Sir, was there a young woman in this cell recently?"

The peasant looked up in astonishment. "The Phantom!"

Raul repeated his query. "Sir, was there a young woman in this cell?"

The peasant nodded. "Aye, sire. A princess she was, sire."

Raul let out his breath in a noisy expression of exasperation. "A princess, sir? Are you certain?"

"Aye, that I am, sire," the man replied. "It was the Princess Cordelia, sire."

"Where did they take her?" Eristan demanded.

The prisoner looked from one man to the other. "I don't know, sires, where they took her. It was Vladimir's men—they rushed in here and took her sudden like. Just a few hours ago, it was."

"And you have no idea where they were taking her?"

A pained expression crossed the man's face. "Nay, sire. I wish I could be of more help, sire."

Raul stepped close to the cell, inserted two thin metal tools into the lock, and fiddled with them for a moment or two. With a loud snap, the lock opened. Raul opened the cell door. "Follow me, sir, but we must make haste." A look of delight swept across the peasant's face as he hurried from the cell. Raul locked the cell door behind him.

Moments later, as the trio emerged from the narrow corridor and slipped into the forest, the moon slipped from behind the clouds, bathing the mountainside with its silvery light. Eristan asked Raul, "What did you do to the guards to render them unconscious?"

Raul grinned and held up the hollow reed. "Poison darts from a blowgun," he replied. "I used a weak solution of extract from the karwac root. The smallest amount will render a man unconscious within seconds and keep him out of commission for ten to fifteen minutes."

Raul turned to the peasant. "You had better make yourself hard to find. Once they discover that you are missing they will come after you again."

"I thank you, sire." The peasant disappeared into the darkness of the forest.

Sir Reginald and Sterling were waiting by a campfire. Looks of dismay swept across their faces as Eristan and Raul approached. "Where's Cordelia?" Sterling blurted.

"She wasn't in the dungeon," Eristan replied, as tears threatened. "They've moved her to another location. Oh, Pa, what are we going to do? We have no idea where they've taken her—how will we ever find her?"

Sir Reginald didn't answer.

Chapter Sixteen

Young King Eristan rubbed the sleep from his eyes and slowly awoke. A songbird's call resounded in the forest, but the cheerful sound never registered. The night had been long and he had gotten very little sleep. The hurried trip to Trandor Castle with Raul had raised his hopes that Cordelia would be found safe and sound, but the discovery that she was no longer in the dungeon had dashed those hopes like a delicate vase hurled against a castle wall. Further rescue attempts would be impossible if her whereabouts were not known. *Where is Cordelia?* he worried. *How will we find her? What will Vladimir demand, and will he return her safely if we meet those demands?*

In his heart, the young king knew exactly what Vladimir's demands would be. Princess Cordelia would be returned only if Eristan ceded the throne of Cheswold to Vladimir, and that he could not do—his father had decreed that he must take the throne at his sixteenth birthday.

He exhaled in a long, noisy sigh of frustration. "Emmanuel, help us," he whispered. "I really do not know what to do. How will we rescue Cordelia if we do not even know her whereabouts?"

His mind went back to a time when life was simpler,

a time when he and his twin sister were nothing more than peasants, supposedly the children of a peasant carpenter, and were known as Dathan and Lanna. He thought of a day when he and Lanna were helping their adopted father around the shop. "Papa," Dathan had asked, "why are we poor? Why are we peasants?"

"What makes you ask that, lad?" Willis had queried.

"I saw Lord Marvin on the road today, riding in his golden carriage. I stood to the side of the road as he passed and I kept my head bowed as you taught us to, but I sneaked a peek at the coach as it passed. His son Geoffrey was looking out the window and I think he saw me. I couldn't help but think about the wonderful life that he has, and then think about how poor we are. Why are we poor when Lord Marvin and his family are so rich?"

"Perhaps King Emmanuel planned it that way," the carpenter had answered. "Are you ashamed of being poor?"

"Oh no, Papa," the little boy had replied quickly. "You taught us that we peasants are just as important to King Emmanuel as the richest of the noblemen."

"Are you dissatisfied with being poor?"

"Nay, Papa, I am content, but I just wish . . . I just wish we could have all the nice things that they have."

"Then you are not content, my son."

Dathan didn't hear him. "Papa, I want to grow up to be a prince. I want to have a horse of my own, and not just any horse, but a magnificent white stallion that would be the finest in the shire. People would stop and look at me as I rode by and they would admire my fine horse."

"Son," Willis had replied, "peasants don't grow up to become princes. Not usually."

"One day I will be a princess," Lanna had decreed. "A

princess with magnificent lace gowns and a castle full of servants to wait on me."

Willis had laughed. "It sounds as if you two are making some grand plans for your future. What if those plans don't come to pass? Will you be happy if you have to live the rest of your lives as peasants?"

"I would rather be a prince, Papa," Dathan had replied.

"Aye, but you are a peasant, not a prin—" Willis had stopped as if to correct himself. "Son, what if you have to live the rest of your life in a humble cottage, working from sunup to sundown, wearing homespun and eating the most meager food—will you be happy?"

Dathan shrugged. "I don't know."

"Remember this, Lanna and Dathan," Willis had urged. "Happiness does not come from having status or possessions. Living a life of luxury in the most magnificent castle in all of Terrestria would not make you happy if you did not serve King Emmanuel. True happiness and fulfillment come only when one serves Emmanuel."

"Papa, why do some people get to be princes or nobles while others have to be peasants? It doesn't seem fair."

Willis shook his head. "I'm not sure, Son, I'm really not sure—"

Just then a voice called at the tent door. "Your Majesty, are you awake, sire?"

Jolted from his reverie, Eristan stretched and yawned. "Aye."

"Breakfast is ready when you are, sire. We have a long ride back to Barrington Castle."

"I'll be ready in minutes," Eristan replied.

King Eristan and his men were saddle weary as they rode across the drawbridge and entered Barrington Castle. "I don't want to see this horse of mine for a month!" the young king told Sir Reginald with a groan as he swung down from the saddle and gave the reins to a stablehand. "Doing a two day ride in one day was a bit too much."

"Aye, Your Majesty, but we are safely back at Barrington," Reginald replied, "and that's what matters. Grab some dinner in the great hall, sire, and then get some sleep. Tomorrow morning you'll be ready for another day."

As the men trudged wearily toward the great hall, Lord Wallace approached Eristan. "Sire, we sent a messenger to try to reach you. Two days ago we received a communication from Vladimir. He sent a list of his demands. Sire, as we suspected, he and his men are still holding the princess."

Eristan sighed. "Let's meet in the council chambers while you show it to me and we decide on a course of action."

"Why not meet in the great hall?" the magistrate suggested. "You and the men can eat while we deal with this."

Eristan nodded. "That would be better. Assemble my cabinet and the High Council at my table, if you would. The knights from the task force can eat at the opposite end of the great hall."

Lord Wallace nodded. "As you wish, sire."

Fifteen minutes later, King Eristan, Sir Reginald, and Sterling dined hungrily on roast duck as the members of the cabinet and the High Council took their places around the table. When all were assembled, Lord Wallace produced a small parchment. "Sire, the communication from the traitor Vladimir."

"Read it aloud as we eat," Eristan ordered.

"Aye, sire, as you wish." The magistrate unrolled the document and began to read aloud. "Young Eristan and the usurpers at Barrington Castle." He looked up from the parchment. "He isn't very respectful, sire."

Eristan shrugged. "I wouldn't expect him to be. Please continue."

"As you know by now," Lord Wallace continued reading, "my men and I have the princess in our custody at an undisclosed location. Please be assured that she is safe and has been treated well, though she seems to resent all of our efforts to make her comfortable. If you will comply with my conditions in a timely manner, my men will escort the princess safely back to Barrington Castle. If not, we will turn her over to the Karnivans to be placed in the custody of Lord Grimlor. In such a case you will be solely responsible for the outcome.

"Eristan, if you wish to affect the safe return of your sister, you must surrender the throne of Cheswold to me immediately. You will then accept the position of Prime Minister of Cheswold, a position which you will hold indefinitely. Captains Vance, Trevarr, and Orwyn will be relieved of their commands, to be replaced by captains of my choosing.

"In the event that you fail to comply with the above conditions, my men and I will not be held responsible for any tragedy that should befall the princess. You have three days to comply." Lord Wallace looked up from the parchment. "It's signed, of course, 'King Vladimir, rightful king of Cheswold'. Your Majesty, I would suggest—"

"It's just as I expected," King Eristan interrupted. "He plans to use Cordelia's life to bargain for the throne."

"What is your response, sire?" one of the captains asked.

The young king shook his head. "We will not respond

immediately. We need time to discuss this and think it through."

"We don't have much time, sire," Lord Wallace told him. "The message was delivered two days ago."

Eristan sighed. "So how do we go about finding Cordelia?"

"In the event that we fail to find her, sire," Captain Vance asked, "do you intend to cede the throne to Vladimir?"

"That is not an option," Eristan snapped. "My father, King William, decreed that I was to take the throne of Cheswold upon my sixteenth birthday. To surrender to Vladimir would be to disobey the dictates of my father, sir, which is something that I simply cannot do. Nay, the only option available to us is to rescue Cordelia."

"That might be easier said than done, sire. We do not know the whereabouts of the princess, and finding her might prove to be impossible."

Eristan ignored the statement. "Gentlemen, how do we go about finding the princess? I am open to suggestions."

"First of all, sire," Captain Vance said, "I would suggest placing roadblocks on the major routes to Karniva and increasing the patrols at the border in hopes of intercepting Cordelia's captors. In the event that Vladimir does decide to deliver her to Grimlor, perhaps we can prevent it."

"I agree," Sir Reginald said. "Roadblocks should be placed immediately."

"We should also quietly send spies posing as minstrels throughout the shires and the castles in hopes of gaining information. Perhaps if a few discreet questions are asked at the right castle, well . . ."

Sterling spoke up. "I would like to volunteer for such duty, sire. I have considerable experience spying in enemy territory, and of course, I have a personal interest in seeing Cordelia return safely to Barrington Castle."

"I'll ask Captains Vance and Trevarr for their best men to serve as spies," the young king replied, "but yes, you may go as a spy. I want as many men as possible to be ready to leave tonight."

"I'm ready now, Eristan. I can leave as soon as I have my assignment."

King Eristan and his cabinet discussed the situation further, making specific plans to increase the number of knights patrolling the border and planning which castles and shires should receive visits from the spies. "I want your best men assembled within the hour," Eristan told the captains. "Our spies must leave the castle tonight."

The next few days were torment for young King Eristan as he paced the royal apartment at Barrington Castle, anxiously awaiting word from his spies. At last, late in the evening of the third day, a sentry rushed in to find him alone on the balcony. "Two of your spies approach the castle, sire," the sentry announced, bowing low. "They ride as men who are eager, and methinks that they bear good tidings."

Eristan's pulse quickened. "Who are they?"

"Unless my eyes deceive me, sire, it looks like Sterling and the tall huntsman."

"Bring them to me immediately."

"Aye, sire." The man bowed low and hurried from the balcony.

Three minutes later, Raul and Sterling stood before King Eristan. "We have found Cordelia," Sterling blurted eagerly. "She is being held prisoner in Marwick Castle, just twelve miles from the Karnivan border. The castle belongs to Lord Marwick, who makes no effort to hide the fact that he is a Karnivan sympathizer."

Eristan's heart beat faster. "Are you certain that it is Cordelia?"

"Aye, we are certain. Raul and I saw her with our own eyes."

"How did you manage that?"

"We were given information that she was being held in Marwick Castle. Posing as locksmiths who had come to service and lubricate the castle locks, we were able to get into the dungeon, but she was not there. After checking the dungeon locks we asked a few discreet questions and learned that Cordelia was being held in the northwest tower of the castle. With a bit of luck we were able to persuade the castle guards to allow us to service the lock on the solar where the princess is being held. As I said, we actually saw her."

Eristan leaned forward eagerly. "How is she? Is she well?"

"She's all right," Sterling replied, "though we could see that her captivity has taken a toll on her."

"Is she in good health?"

"Aye, from what we could see."

"How well did you check out the castle defenses? How difficult would it be to accomplish a rescue?"

"It would not be impossible," Raul replied, "but it would be extremely difficult. The castle is on high alert. Sentries not only patrol the outer curtains, but the barbicans and baileys as well. The tower itself was guarded by four sentries. We were accompanied by two sentries with loaded crossbows who kept us under observation the entire time that we were in the vicinity of the tower."

Eristan was pleased. "Well, we've taken the first step in rescuing Cordelia," he exulted. "We've actually located her."

Raul cleared his throat. "Sire, with Emmanuel's help all things are possible, of course, but attempting to rescue a prisoner from Marwick Castle will be no easy task. Sentries were everywhere and they watched us like hawks the entire time that we were in the castle. It was almost as if they anticipated that we were planning a rescue attempt. Sire, rescuing the princess will prove to be no easy task. Nothing is impossible, of course, but this does come mighty close."

"You've seen the castle and the tower and you've had a day or so to think about it," Sir Reginald spoke up. "If you were to attempt to rescue Princess Cordelia, just how would you go about it?"

"A direct assault on the castle would be a mistake," Sterling said, and Raul nodded in agreement. "The castle defenses are well-planned. The castle has a double gatehouse and the portcullis is down at all times. Apparently, they raise it once each hour if residents are seeking entrance or egress."

Eristan frowned. "They're not making this easy for us, are they?"

"Well, sire, they are holding the princess hostage and I'm sure that they anticipate a rescue attempt. We should not be surprised that extra security measures are in place. Actually, I expected nothing less."

"It was rumored that Vladimir and his men are headquartered in Marwick Castle," Sterling said, "but we saw none of his men during our brief visit and we chose not to investigate for fear of arousing suspicions."

The young king nodded. "Very well. I would have done the same." He looked from Sterling to Raul and then back again. "You've seen the castle defenses and you've seen the tower where my sister is being held. How would you suggest that we proceed?"

"I agree with Sterling," Raul began. "A direct assault on the castle would be a huge mistake, as it can only end in failure and might even result in the death of the princess. The only feasible way to rescue her would be at night, under the cover of darkness. I would suggest that we construct a special raft to cross the moat and devise some way to secure it to the base of the outer curtain. A team of knights could then scale the outer curtain, cross the barbican, and then scale the inner curtain and gain access to the tower." He paused. "Sire, I am prepared to lead such a force."

Eristan's pulse quickened. "How many men would you take?"

"Six, including myself," the huntsman replied. "They and six other men could easily carry a raft that would support the six. After launching the raft, the six extra men would lie low and provide cover for the rescue force when they returned with the princess."

Eristan sighed. "Please be honest with me, sir. What are our chances of success?"

"Slim, sire, very slim," Raul replied quietly. "And yet, I see no other option."

The young king nodded. "Cordelia must be rescued, and I see no other way. Let's get some sleep and we'll start planning first thing in the morning."

Chapter Seventeen

The night was dark. King Eristan and his men crouched in the thickets and windbreaks on the ridge overlooking Marwick Castle as they anxiously awaited the return of the rescue force. A cold breeze swept in from the north, rustling the reeds and branches and creating a restless, uneasy feeling in the depths of Eristan's soul. Lifting a spyglass to his eye, he studied the castle battlements, hoping to see the men returning with Cordelia.

"They've been gone more than an hour, sire," a tall, nervous knight offered. "Perchance something has gone wrong—"

"Nothing has gone wrong," the young king growled, though in his heart he was not so certain. "Raul and Sterling know what they are doing. They're moving slowly to avoid detection. We saw Raul take out both sentries with his blow gun. I'm certain that they will return with Princess Cordelia at any moment now."

The moon peeked from behind a cloud, brightening the outer castle curtain until it gleamed like silver. Eristan groaned. "Stay hidden," he implored the moon. "We don't need you right now." As if in response, the moon abruptly retreated again, plunging Marwick Castle into darkness. Eristan let out a sigh of relief.

"Sire, I see something," another knight said in a low voice. "I see figures on the sentrywalk."

Eristan studied the castle through the glass. "I see nothing."

At that moment a shout echoed through the darkness and several dark figures raced along the sentrywalk toward the north tower. The moon darted from behind the clouds, bathing the entire castle in its silvery beams, and the figures on the wall could now be clearly seen. Eristan's heart leaped as he saw that one of the figures was a woman with long, golden tresses. "It's Sterling and Raul!" the young king exulted. "And they have Cordelia with them! Praise be to Emmanuel!"

As Eristan and his men watched, three Marwick knights charged along the sentrywalk toward Cordelia and her rescuers. The stillness of the night was shattered by the sound of sword striking sword as a fierce battle ensued. Within moments, all three Marwick knights lay motionless upon the battlements. Eristan's men cheered softly.

"Sterling, get out of there," Eristan muttered. "Get Cordelia out of there."

Just then a score of Marwick knights swarmed up the stairs and charged across the sentrywalk. With lusty cries of rage they threw themselves upon the invaders. "Our men are hopelessly outnumbered," one of Eristan's knights moaned. The young king and his men watched helplessly.

A figure shrouded in white leaped from the castle wall, sailed through the darkness of the night, and landed in the moat with a splash. "It's the princess!" Eristan's men exclaimed. "She jumped!" At that moment, Cordelia's six rescuers leaped from the battlements to land in the moat beside her.

"Charge the castle!" King Eristan shouted, leaping from his hiding place and rushing down the hill. "Archers, take out the men on the wall!"

As the Barrington knights raced down the slope after their king, archers appeared atop the curtain of Marwick castle with longbows in their hands. Before they could fire the first shot, however, a barrage of arrows flew upwards from the ranks of Eristan's men, dropping a handful of Marwick men with the first volley.

Eristan and his men reached the castle moat at the same moment as Cordelia and her rescuers touched the bank. A volley of arrows rained down upon them, hitting two of the Barrington men and killing one. Leaning down, Eristan seized Cordelia by the arms and dragged her from the moat. "Run to the hills," he ordered, pointing.

The drawbridge thundered down with the clatter of chains and the whirr of pulleys, and a garrison of armed knights charged out to engage King Eristan and his men. "Fight for Cheswold and King Emmanuel!" Eristan cried, drawing his sword and rushing forward. In a moment's time, the battle was joined.

A short, stout knight leaped at Eristan, swinging his sword with both hands. The young king side-stepped, deflecting the blow with the blade of his own sword and throwing the enemy knight off balance. Eristan lunged at the man, striking him squarely in the breastplate with his shoulder. The man staggered backwards, giving Eristan time to recover and bring his sword into play. In a moment, the man lay motionless upon the ground, mortally wounded.

A cry of rage caused Eristan to spin to his left just in time to see a broadsword flashing toward his face. He twisted away sharply but knew in that instant that it was too late. There was no time to avoid the deadly blow. As he tried desperately to raise his shield to fend off the blade, a bolt of fear shot through him and he braced himself for the searing pain that he knew would result. Suddenly he was hurled forward and a heavy CLANG sounded in his ear.

He fell, twisting sideways as he did, and looked up to see a flashing sword deflect the deadly blow intended for him. He hit the ground hard but rolled to his feet immediately, sword still in hand, ready for battle. The Barrington knight who had come to his rescue was fighting hard, swinging his sword with furious abandon and driving Eristan's assailant before him. The Marwick knight turned to flee, but the Barrington man ended his life.

The Barrington knight turned and Eristan saw his face. "Sterling! You saved my life!"

"'Twas an honor, my king," Sterling replied. "Eristan, we have to get Cordelia out of here."

A cavalcade of mounted knights came thundering across the drawbridge with swords drawn and bore down in fury upon the Barrington knights. "To the hills, men!" Eristan cried. He spun around, searching desperately for Cordelia. To his dismay, she was in the grip of two Marwick men who were dragging her back toward the castle.

"Sterling, help me!" Eristan cried, running toward his sister. Sterling was right on his heels.

"Release the lady," Eristan ordered the two men. "I am your king." Cordelia's captors released her immediately but turned to fight. Sterling sprang forward, positioning himself between Cordelia and the men. Both Marwick men turned on him, slashing furiously with their swords.

"Stay behind me," Eristan told his sister as he leaped forward to assist Sterling. Shoulder to shoulder, Eristan and Sterling fought desperately against the two Marwick knights, but the enemy knights were strong and skilled in the use of the sword. "This is where Melzar's training will come into play,"

Eristan grunted, wielding his sword with two hands to block a vicious horizontal cut. The Marwick knight was fast and relentless, and the powerful blows came in rapid succession.

"Your Majesty, the situation does not look good," Sterling panted, working swiftly with his own sword to repel the attacks of his adversary. "Our forces are outnumbered four to one."

"Aye," Eristan gasped, as he parried a lightning quick series of combinations. "I should have brought an entire battalion, but I wanted to travel fast and light."

"What are we going to do?" his friend asked, leaping to one side to avoid a thrust of the enemy's sword and then darting in to deal a mortal blow of his own. The Marwick man went down. "If we stay here our men will be slaughtered and Cordelia will be recaptured."

Swinging his sword furiously, the young king drove his assailant backward. Sterling leaped in to help, and within moments, felled the other Marwick knight. At that moment, Raul reached him. "Your Majesty, our men are being slaughtered. We're hopelessly outnumbered, sire."

A flash of white caught King Eristan's attention and he turned to see the Dove circle once overhead with the gentle admonition, "Have your men follow me." As he watched, the celestial bird flew swiftly into a nearby canyon.

"Retreat!" the young king called, pointing. "Into that canyon!"

Raul grabbed his elbow in an effort to get his attention. "Your Majesty, that's a blind canyon! The Marwick men will cut us off and we'll be trapped! We'll be slaughtered like sheep!"

"Trust me; I know what I am doing," Eristan replied. He raised his voice again. "Men of Barrington, retreat! Retreat into the canyon!"

The moon seemed to glow even brighter as the Barrington

knights followed their young king into the narrow canyon. Eristan caught a glimpse of white at the far end of the canyon and hurried toward it with Cordelia and Sterling right beside him. "Hurry!" he cried. "To the far end of the canyon!"

Seeing their quarry escaping into the canyon, the Marwick knights regrouped and then stalked slowly to the mouth of the chasm with expressions of triumph evident on their moonlit faces. Grinning broadly, they slowly advanced toward the trapped Barrington knights. The Marwick cavalry waited at the canyon entrance.

"It's hopeless," Sterling groaned. "There's no escape! They'll take us captive or slaughter us like so many pigs."

"I'm following the directions of the Dove," King Eristan replied quietly as a gentle peace flooded his soul. "Perhaps King Emmanuel has provided a way of escape."

A howling gust of wind swept down from the peaks above, powerful and chilling. The canyon trembled. A white-hot bolt of lightning slashed from the heavens and struck the ridge above the canyon. Thunder roared. The mountain shook and the rocks trembled. With a roaring cacophony of sound that made it seem as if all of Terrestria were being destroyed, the mountain collapsed. The side of the canyon fell away, sliding downward with a thunderous roar and forever sealing off the entrance to the canyon. The air was suddenly filled with a thick cloud of dust as the Marwick knights disappeared.

Moments later, an unearthly silence prevailed, ominous in its intensity. As the dust began to settle, the moon once again became visible. "W-What happened?" Cordelia cried.

"King Emmanuel provided a way of escape," her brother said simply. "Most of the Marwick knights were buried in the rockslide."

"What a horrible way to die," Cordelia sobbed.

Eristan sighed. "They were my people," he replied quietly. "Though they were disloyal to the throne, they were still my people."

Raul appeared at his elbow. "If we stay against the eastern wall I think we can cross the rockslide safely. As far as I can tell, the few remaining Marwick knights have fled to the castle."

Early the next morning, King Eristan and Princess Cordelia rode triumphantly up the approach to Barrington Castle while the cavalcade of Barrington knights marched proudly behind them. Apparently, news of Cordelia's rescue had reached the castle, for the roadway was flanked on both sides with throngs of cheering people while the battlements were lined with grinning knights. "Hail the princess!" a man shouted, and the crowd roared its approval and then took up the cry. "Hail the princess!"

Eristan turned to Cordelia. "They're glad you're safely home," he said quietly. "And so am I."

As the triumphant rescue party passed beneath the portcullis, the young king heard someone calling to get his attention. "Your Majesty! Your Majesty!" Eristan turned to see Lord Wallace waving frantically. "Your Majesty, I simply must speak with you."

King Eristan dismounted and turned the mare over to a stablehand. Lord Wallace rushed forward. "Your Majesty, Captains Vance and Orwyn must meet with you immediately. Vladimir is attacking the castles, sire, and Grimlor's forces are massing on the Karnivan border. They're preparing to invade Cheswold, sire."

Eristan was stunned. "But we're not ready."

The Chief Magistrate nodded. "Aye, sire, that we know, and no one knows that better than Vladimir. We think that his men are laying siege to several castles in order to tie up those garrisons of knights and keep them from coming to the defense of Barrington Castle."

"Barrington Castle?" Eristan echoed slowly.

"Aye, sire. Our scouts tell us that ten Karnivan battalions are preparing to march on the castle. Grimlor intends to seize the throne, sire. This is the invasion that Cheswold has long feared, and yet we are not prepared."

Chapter Eighteen

King Eristan watched as Captain Orwyn's thick finger touched the map. "Grimlor's forces are assembled right here in the Forest of Ruan, sire, south of Xanterra. It's a very secluded location, more than half a day's march from the border. Apparently, Grimlor is planning a surprise attack, but our spies located his troops and alerted us to his plans."

"What makes you think that Grimlor plans to march on Barrington Castle?" Sir Reginald asked.

"Again, it's simply based on information we received from our spies, but it fits the picture." The captain began touching various locations on the map. "Vladimir is attacking Garlock Castle here, and Ruan Castle here, Silvington Castle here, and Lithium Castle here. Do you see the pattern? Vladimir is engaging only those castles that lie close to Grimlor's route from the Karnivan border to Barrington Castle. It all fits, sire. I really believe that Grimlor is preparing to attack Barrington."

Eristan nodded. "I follow your reasoning. What are our options?"

Captain Orwyn sighed. "I would suggest that we try to capture Vladimir, sire. If we can take him out and squelch the revolution, possibly we would regain the two battalions for the battle against Grimlor."

"How would we take Vladimir?"

The captain touched the map. "Vladimir took Lithium Castle yesterday, and we believe that he is still there. If we could retake the castle—"

"Vladimir took the castle?" Eristan interrupted. "What happened to the residents?"

"He imprisoned the Lithium knights, of course," the captain replied, "but he released the residents without harm."

Eristan gave a sigh of relief. "That's good news."

Sir Reginald spoke up. "How would you go about attacking Lithium Castle?"

Captain Orwyn paused. "Captains Vance, Trevarr, and I need to study on it, of course, but I would almost be tempted to use the Ai strategy."

"The Ai strategy? What is that?"

The captain grinned. "Remember the story of the city of Ai, from Terrestria's ancient history? Joshua attacked the city with a small force. The men of Ai, anticipating a quick, easy victory, opened the city gates and pursued Joshua's men. Joshua had a much larger force lying in wait and they quickly took the city."

"Would that strategy work with Vladimir?"

The captain slowly nodded. "It very well might. Vladimir is quite vain and considers himself a brilliant battle strategist, though he actually knows very little about warfare. If he sensed a quick, seemingly safe victory, I daresay that he might decide to lead his men in person. If so, he would walk right into our trap."

King Eristan looked at the other two captains. "Gentlemen, what do you think? Would the Ai strategy work against Lithium Castle?"

Captain Orwyn nodded. "Sire, it's very simplistic, but it has been successful more than once. Aye, I believe that it could work, especially if we gave Vladimir some compelling reason to come out against us."

Sir Reginald frowned. "Such as?"

The captain shrugged. "I don't know, sir."

Eristan chuckled. "What if Vladimir thought that he could take *me* captive? What if I were to ride against Lithium Castle with a small force, say, just a few dozen men?"

Captain Orwyn shook his head. "It's too risky, sire. I don't like the idea of using you as bait."

"We want to give Vladimir a compelling reason to come out against us," Eristan replied evenly. "The possibility of my capture would be that compelling reason. I am willing to ride against the castle if you think my presence might draw him out."

"Let's have a decoy ride in your place, sire. We can dress another knight in your armor and allow him to display your coat of arms. That would be safer and yet accomplish the same goal."

"Such a plan would place that knight in danger," the young king growled, "and also convince my men that I am a coward at heart. Nay, gentlemen, the only knight to ride into battle with my coat of arms will be me."

"I still don't like the idea of using you as bait, Your Majesty," Captain Orwyn said, shaking his head. "It's just too risky."

Eristan grinned at him. "Then just make sure that you and your men do a good job of protecting me," he said with a laugh. He grew serious. "I like the idea of using the Ai strategy to draw Vladimir out. Let's plan the attack right now . . . ."

Later that evening Eristan walked with Cordelia on the balcony. "So we leave tonight for Lithium Castle," he told her. "Our spies are convinced that Vladimir is there and we intend to try to draw him out to be captured. Once we take Vladimir and secure the castle, I will try to convince Captains Alexander and Randor to return the two errant battalions to my command. Once that is accomplished, our combined forces will then march northward to challenge the Karnivan invasion."

He squeezed her hand. "Cordelia, I'm sorry that I had to rush into that meeting. We haven't had time to talk." He took a deep breath and turned to face her. "How were you treated by Vladimir's men?"

She shuddered. "They weren't cruel or unkind, but still, it was a horrible experience. I didn't know what they intended to do with me and I worried about what you were going through. I figured that Vladimir was going to use me to force you to relinquish the throne and I didn't want you to do that. When I saw Sterling the first time, it gave me hope that I would be rescued, and then they moved me to prevent that." She smiled sadly. "That was really discouraging."

He hugged her. "You cannot imagine the anguish in my soul when I learned that you had been taken hostage. My first thought was to give up the throne to get you back safely, for I was sure that was what Vladimir had in mind when his men seized you."

She gave him a strange look. "It wasn't Vladimir's men who captured me."

"Then who was it?"

Cordelia snorted. "It was Sir Winston. He was terribly

upset when you removed him from being the constable of Barrington Castle, you know, and he captured me to get even with you. Once he had me, of course, he turned me over to Vladimir in hopes of getting in Vladimir's good graces should Vladimir be successful in his attempts to retake the throne."

"Sir Winston shall hang for this," King Eristan declared. "A traitor such as he does not deserve to live."

He hugged her again. "I am thankful that you are safe. I was so worried."

The waning moon etched the battlements of Lithium Castle with gleaming silver as two battalions of the army of Cheswold moved silently into position in the hills surrounding the castle. Once the battalions were in place, one hundred carefully chosen knights followed King Eristan down a draw that led to the moor in front of the castle approach. The plan was simple. Once the drawbridge was lowered for the day, Cheswoldian knights disguised as farmers would attempt to immobilize the drawbridge with large wooden wedges while others would block the portcullis open with two large beams. Eristan himself would then lead an attack against the castle gates with a paltry force of a few dozen men in hopes of drawing Vladimir from the castle. If Vladimir responded by leading a charge against Eristan's men, the rest of the two battalions would rush in from the forest in hopes of cutting Vladimir off from the castle.

The young king settled in for the remainder of the night on a patch of thick grass and then sent a petition to King Emmanuel. As he closed his eyes, hoping to get two or three hours' sleep before daybreak, a cricket somewhere beneath his bedroll began to chirp with all the enthusiasm of a youth at a jousting tournament. At last, Eristan's anxious thoughts quieted and he slept fitfully.

It seemed just moments later that someone was shaking his elbow and calling softly, "Your Majesty, wake up—it's time to take positions. The hay wagon is in place in the woods, ready to be driven to the front gate as soon as the portcullis goes up. We're ready, sire."

The young king opened his eyes to look up into the face of Sir Reginald. "Can't we do this another day?" Eristan groaned. "I'm not ready to get up just yet."

Reginald laughed softly. "Most of us feel the same way, my lord, but we're ready to deal with Vladimir once and for all. Perhaps you can sleep in tomorrow, sire."

Eristan grimaced as he rolled to his feet. "Let's plan on it." He looked around the makeshift camp as various knights slipped silently from their bedrolls. "How much longer till sunrise?"

"We figure about forty minutes, sire. It's going to start getting light soon, sire, and we need to get the men into position."

An hour later the sun was up and steadily burning the mists from the moors and fells. The castle portcullis had been raised and the drawbridge was down, allowing a handful of merchants to enter the castle and a few travelers to leave. The sentries paid no attention to an elderly farmer driving a heavily loaded hay wagon up the castle approach. An alert observer would have noticed that the team of four horses was far more spirited than ordinary farm horses.

The hay wagon approached the drawbridge. As the farmer pulled his team to the side of the approach, four men seemed to drop from the sides of the wagon. Snatching long timbers from the sides of the wagon, two of them raced across the drawbridge and propped the portcullis open while their two companions immobilized the drawbridge by driving large wedges into the joint of the bridge. Dashing back across the drawbridge, the four men leaped aboard the farm wagon, which took off like a rabbit pursued by hounds.

"Let's go, men!" King Eristan's heart was in his throat as he mounted the mare and spurred her forward. As he reached the head of the draw, forty pikemen and forty archers followed him, dashing across the moor and racing up the castle approach where a battering ram was already waiting on a second farm wagon. The pikemen seized the battering ram and raced across the drawbridge while the archers took up positions along the edge of the moat and unleashed a volley of arrows over the castle walls. Twenty mounted Barrington knights rode forward and joined King Eristan as he rode along the edge of the moat, alert for enemy arrows.

A barrage of arrows rained down upon Eristan's knights and men began to fall. Raul rode forward. "Sire, we're losing men fast. May I respectfully suggest, sire, that we withdraw and move beyond arrow range. If this continues, we'll all be dead men."

Eristan nodded. "Quite right." He stood in the stirrups and bellowed, "Retreat, men! Follow me!"

Wheeling the mare about, he galloped toward the shelter of the hills. As the men regrouped around him, his heart sank when he saw how many men had been injured. The operation was costing far more lives than he had imagined. "Emmanuel, help us," he breathed. "Should we continue, or should we abandon this as folly?"

"We shan't win this, sire," a knight remarked. "Why do we not engage all our men and attack the castle in force?"

"This entire operation is a ruse," the young king told him, speaking loudly enough for the group around him to hear. "We purposely attacked with a small force in an attempt to provoke Vladimir to chase us. If we can draw Vladimir and his men from the safety of the castle, we can perhaps capture him and end the rebellion." He sighed. "We didn't realize that we would lose this many men."

Raul spoke up. "What now, sire?"

"We'll move against the castle again," Eristan told him, "but we'll stop just out of arrow range. Perhaps our presence will provoke Vladimir to attack us."

"Shall we replace the men we lost?"

Eristan shook his head. "We're trying to create the impression that I came against Lithium Castle with a small force. If we bring replacements, Vladimir will know that we have more men." He swept the group with a quick glance. "If Vladimir does indeed ride against us, here's what we will do." The men listened intently as he gave brief instructions for a maneuver to confuse the enemy.

He turned the mare. "Ready, men? Let's ride."

King Eristan and the company of Cheswoldian knights rode slowly up the castle approach. "The gate is opening, sire!" a knight called softly. "Perhaps the plan is working!"

"Company, halt," Eristan ordered.

The huge gates of Lithium Castle were indeed opening. As Eristan and his men watched, a huge warrior rode onto the drawbridge, followed by a company of mounted knights. "Vladimir!" Eristan breathed. "It's working!"

"Prepare to attack," he said softly. "Wait for my signal."

The young king waited until Vladimir and his men were less than eighty yards away. "Ready? Attack, now!" Spurring his horse, he and a dozen men charged straight for Vladimir's company while the rest of his men wheeled their horses and dashed for the draw where the rest of the Cheswoldian army waited in ambush.

Just as planned, one of Eristan's knights looked backward over his shoulder and then cried, "Sire, retreat! Our men are abandoning us!"

On cue, Eristan looked over his shoulder and then cried, "Retreat!" He wheeled his horse with the others and dashed for the draw.

Vladimir couldn't resist. Throwing caution to the winds, he stood in the stirrups and cried, "After them, men! Charge!"

The battle was over almost before it started. In pursuit of Eristan, Vladimir and his men rounded the hillock and rode at full gallop into the draw, and then realized at the last second that they had ridden into a trap. Vladimir wheeled his horse in a hasty attempt to retreat, but an archer's arrow caught him in the throat and he tumbled from the saddle. Reining their mounts to a halt and throwing their hands into the air, his men immediately surrendered. The army of Cheswold disarmed Vladimir's men and marched them back into the castle.

King Eristan rode into the bailey and sat astride his magnificent white mare, watching in silence as the prisoners were marched across the courtyard and down to the dungeons. The Lithium knights had just been released, and they helped secure the new occupants in their cells.

With a look of satisfaction on his face, Sterling approached Eristan. "We found this on Vladimir's body, sire. My guess is that Sir Winston stole it and surrendered it to him."

Eristan's heart leaped as Sterling handed him the golden dagger.

Chapter Nineteen

Captain Vance reined his horse close to King Eristan's mare and rode alongside. "My scouts tell me that the Karnivans are preparing to invade within the next day or two, sire. The battle will go much easier if we can intercept them at the border rather than battle them in the lowlands."

Eristan sat straighter in the saddle. "How far are we from the border?"

"Less than half a day's march, sire. At present we're approximately six miles due north of Xanterra."

Eristan's heart leaped. "Xanterra? The Forbidden City?"

"Aye, sire."

"But I thought the pass at Xanterra was blocked."

"Aye, sire, that is correct. It is quite impassible. Our route will take us west of Xanterra to another mountain pass a few miles further."

A strange emotion stirred within the young king's breast and he suddenly he felt a compelling urge to enter the Forbidden City. Deep within his soul it seemed that a voice from the past was calling him, wooing him, urging him to come, and though he was riding to battle to save Cheswold, he found that he couldn't resist. He turned in the saddle and surveyed the two battalions marching behind him and then turned back to face Captain Vance. "How much time would we lose if we go by way of Xanterra?"

"There's no such route, sire. As you know, the mountain pass is forever closed. If we were to march to Xanterra, we would simply retrace our steps as we make our way to the border. We cannot afford the time, sire."

"The cavalry travels far faster than the infantry," Eristan replied. "What if I were to take a division of the cavalry to Xanterra and then double back to meet the rest of the forces? We would lose no time."

Captain Vance was puzzled. "For what purpose, sire?"

Eristan shook his head as if to clear his thoughts. "I—I really don't know, Captain. Something within me tells me to go to Xanterra, and go immediately. I cannot explain it, but, it's—it's as if a voice is telling me—no, ordering me—ordering me to go to Xanterra. Sir, I must go to the Forbidden City."

The captain was obviously perplexed. "Perhaps His Majesty could make such a visit to the Forbidden City at another time. Grimlor is preparing to invade, sire, and this is not the time to make an excursion to Xanterra."

The young king shook his head. "I must go now, Captain. Give me twenty of your best men and we will ride immediately for Xanterra. We can catch up before the infantry nears the border."

"If I may be so bold as to speak, sire, I would not—"

"Captain."

The officer bowed slightly. "As you wish, sire. Twenty cavalrymen, sire. Right away. sire. Please ride with caution, Your Majesty."

Nearly an hour later, a light, cold rain drizzled down as King Eristan and his entourage of cavalrymen rode slowly through a rugged canyon. Tall, jagged spires of ironstone rose on both sides like the blades of enormous swords. Sterling spurred his horse and darted forward to ride alongside Eristan, glancing anxiously upward at the towering spires. "This place is eerie, isn't it? This looks like a good place for an ambush."

Eristan shrugged as he eyed the soaring formations and then the narrow track before them. "There would be no way to scale the walls and there are no real hiding places."

"True," Sterling replied, "but something about this place just screams 'Danger!' I felt this premonition the moment we entered the canyon. Don't you feel it? It's as if we're being watched, and something really bad is about to happen."

"There is something about this chasm that is a bit unsettling," the young king admitted, "but I'm sure it's just our imaginations."

"Unsettling?" Sterling echoed. "I'd hardly call it unsettling. Right now every hair on the back of my neck is standing straight up."

"Your mind is playing tricks on you because of all the legends about Xanterra," Eristan replied. "Relax. We won't stay long."

Moments later the riders entered Xanterra. Vacant buildings flanked both sides of the trail, and they were the most unusual structures that Eristan had ever seen. Carved from solid rock, the two- and three-story buildings extended into the mountain itself. Windows and doors were missing, and the empty openings stared at the riders like lifeless eyes and gaping mouths.

Eristan jumped as a raucous screech echoed across the defile. He looked up just as a large, hideous bird took wing and soared down the canyon. A cold finger of fear traced a line down his back. *Sterling is right,* he thought. *This place is unnerving.*

"This is as far as we come, Your Majesty," one of the cavalrymen called. "Look."

Jolted from his reverie, King Eristan looked up to see that an enormous rockslide blocked the canyon. A jumble of boulders, some as big as hay wagons, obstructed their passage. A stone wall was visible in the rubble. Eristan rode forward and spotted the edge of an iron portcullis. "Xanterra Castle," he said. "The rockslide struck it directly."

The men dismounted and surveyed the remains of the castle. "Nobody in the castle had a chance," one knight said soberly. "The mountain came thundering down on them and buried them in an instant."

"Look, Your Majesty, the earthquake opened the dungeon," another knight said, emerging from a fissure under the rocks. "Any prisoners down there were buried alive."

"Stand where you are!" a harsh voice demanded. "If just one of you makes a sudden move your leader gets a bolt right through the heart!"

Eristan and his men looked up to see a tattered figure on the rocks above them. Skeletal hands gripped a loaded crossbow, which was aimed directly at the young king's heart. "You," the figure ordered, indicating Eristan with a small thrust of the deadly weapon, "don't move a muscle until I give the word. The rest of you mount up slowly and ride out of here without looking back. Once you are out of Xanterra I will release your leader and he can catch up to you."

Eristan slowly raised both hands, lifted his eyes to the thin, gray-robed figure, and was startled to realize that it was a woman. "We mean you no harm, my good woman," he said in a gentle, reassuring voice. "I am King Eristan. My men and I just came for a brief look at Xanterra. We will leave at once."

"You lie, sir," the woman snarled, and the crossbow jerked

violently. "Young Eristan is dead. He and the princess were killed on the night that Barrington Castle was taken by the Karnivans." The woman's voice quavered as she said the words.

"I am Eristan," the young king insisted. "Princess Cordelia and I were taken to a place of safety by Sir Reginald on the night my father died defending Barrington Castle. I took the throne from Vladimir just weeks ago."

"That's impossible!" The woman spat out the words.

"I am sorry that we have bothered you, good woman," Eristan said quietly. "Now, if you'll permit us, my men and I will leave quietly."

The crossbow never wavered. "Not so quickly, sir. I want you to prove that you are Prince Eristan, son of King William of Cheswold."

Still facing the deadly crossbow, Eristan felt a surge of anger. "What do you seek, woman?"

"The prince had a birthmark on the back of his right knee," the woman challenged. "Show your knee, sir."

Eristan was stunned. "What?"

"If you are indeed Prince Eristan, sir, you should have the birthmark behind your knee."

The young king took a deep breath to control his surging anger, stood in the stirrups, and ripped open his right legging. Turning slowly away from the peasant woman, he showed her the back of his knee.

"Emmanuel be praised, you *are* Prince Eristan!" The woman was so overwhelmed that she dropped the crossbow, which fired the bolt, striking one of the horses in the leg. The animal reared up, screaming in terror, and it took several men to get him under control.

Sobbing uncontrollably, the woman clambered down the face of the rockslide, mumbling over and over, "Prince Eristan!

You really are Prince Eristan!" Reaching up, she seized Eristan's right leg with dirty, gnarled hands and leaned her head against his boot. "Eristan! Oh, Eristan! The last time I saw you and Cordelia . . ." Overcome with emotion, the peasant woman collapsed against the horse.

Eristan's men pulled her away and the young king dismounted. "Who are you, woman?"

Sobbing, the woman looked up at him. "My name is Martha. I was your nurse at Barrington Castle."

Stunned, Eristan found that he could not even breathe. Looking into the guileless eyes that studied his face so eagerly, he knew at once that the old woman was telling the truth. He reached for her.

Martha stepped back. "Sire, one prisoner still lives, though buried beneath the castle. I have fed him for fourteen years. Will you and your men free him?"

A strange, powerful emotion stirred deep within Eristan's soul. "Martha, show us where to find him."

"Follow me." In an instant, the woman disappeared into the fissure beneath the rock pile. Sterling and Eristan and one other knight followed her cautiously. They found her in a dimly lit underground chamber, kneeling at the edge of a large, flat boulder that leaned precariously against a stone wall. As they approached, she thrust her hand into a large void beneath the boulder.

"An underground stream provides him with water and carries away waste, and I slide food to him each morning and evening. His mind is gone and he hasn't spoken in years, but I know that he is alive, for he passes the food bowl back out each time." Even in the poor light Eristan could see that her face was wet with tears. "The last few weeks, Prince Eristan, he has been very ill, for I hear him coughing each day, and the cough is steadily getting worse. Will you and your men get him out?"

The young king was astounded at what he had just heard. "You have been taking care of this poor man for fourteen years?" he asked, incredulous.

"Aye," Martha replied. "Ever since he was imprisoned here at Xanterra."

Eristan was puzzled. "But why did you not seek help to rescue this poor man?"

She hesitated. "There was too much danger," she replied at last. "I couldn't risk having the news get back to Vladimir that he was still alive."

Eristan suddenly found that he could not even breathe. "Who . . . who is this man?" he managed.

"The prisoner is King William, ruler of Cheswold. Prince Eristan, your father is still alive."

Chapter Twenty

King Eristan studied the bearded, emaciated old man who lay on the pallet before him. Lifeless eyes stared back at him, unresponsive and unseeing, and Eristan thought at first that his father was blind, but when Martha silently entered the tent that had been pitched as a temporary shelter, the eyes darted in that direction. "How long—" Eristan choked on the words and he had to try again. "How long has he been like this? He hasn't spoken once."

"He hasn't spoken in the last five or six years," the elderly nurse replied, "but his mind was gone even before that. When your mother died, the grief overwhelmed him and we knew that he was losing his mind, but it was kept quiet at Barrington Castle. At times, he was quite lucid and he realized what was happening to him. He began to make plans to install Vladimir as regent when he himself became unable to govern properly, but those plans were kept secret from the people."

"But I read the document that he prepared on the night Barrington Castle was taken," Eristan protested. "That was certainly written by a sane man."

Martha nodded. "As I said, he had good days and bad days. When it became obvious that Barrington would fall to the

Karnivans, his first thought was for your safety, and he arranged for Sir Reginald and his wife to take you into hiding. Shortly after you left the castle, word came that you had all been killed by the Karnivans. Overcome with grief, King William lost his mind completely."

"But how did he end up in the dungeon at Xanterra?"

"Vladimir wanted him out of the way, but didn't have the heart to kill him, I suppose. He spread the rumor that William was killed in the battle for the castle, and everyone believed it."

"How did you find out that he was still alive?" Eristan asked. "How did you find him at Xanterra?"

"I followed Vladimir's men when they took your father to Xanterra," Martha replied fiercely. "Once I knew that he was imprisoned, I begged the members of the royal court to rescue your father, but my tales seemed to be the ravings of a lunatic, I imagine, and no one would believe me. I returned to Xanterra and the dungeon guards allowed me to bring food to your father once each day."

"And when the earthquake and rockslide destroyed Xanterra, you discovered that he was still alive and continued to bring him food."

"Actually, I was in the dungeon corridor when the rockslide took place," she replied quietly. "It took me five days to dig myself out."

Eristan was astounded. "What about the other prisoners?"

"They were buried in such ways that I could not get to them," she replied sadly. "Emmanuel be praised, I could still bring food to my king."

The young king marveled at the heroic tale. A violent fit of coughing interrupted his thoughts and he turned to watch the pathetic figure on the pallet curl into a fetal position, his body racked with coughs.

A tall knight entered the tent at that moment. "Your Majesty, a lookout reports that the royal coach was spotted in the valley below. The princess will be here in about five minutes, sire."

Eristan nodded. "Very well. What news of the Karnivans?"

"The scouts report that they haven't begun to move yet, sire, though their preparations seem complete and they could march at any moment. We believe that they are awaiting more troops from the south. Captain Orwyn is waiting to speak to you, sire."

"Show him in."

As Captain Orwyn entered the tent, the strain was evident in his face. "Grimlor could invade at any moment, sire, and the army looks to you for leadership. Your Majesty, will you lead us against the Karnivans before they strike against us?"

The young king shook his head. "I shall not leave my father."

"But what about Cheswold? I can lead the men into battle, sire, but they will fight better if you are present. We need you, sire."

"As I said, I shall stay with my father."

"And what of the battle, sire? Shall I lead our armies against Karniva?"

"Not yet," the young king replied. "I want one day with my father and then I shall lead Cheswold's armies against the Karnivans."

The captain bowed. "As you wish, sire." Bowing again, he backed from the tent.

Eristan turned to Martha. "Sterling was given a parchment by a peasant. It had a map of a castle drawn in invisible writing and it had a cryptic message about a lion crouching deep and a treasure far from the keep. Did you send that message to Sterling?"

The old woman nodded. "My son delivered it. We had heard that a new, young king had taken the throne from Vladimir, although we did not know that it was you. I dared not send a message saying that King William was still alive for fear that it would fall into the wrong hands. King William loved riddles and was very good at them, so I thought that perhaps the new king would decipher the message and come to Xanterra."

"The 'lion' refers to my father, but what about the 'treasure'? What was that?"

"The crown jewels, of course," she replied. "Your father had them with him."

Eristan was incredulous. "My father had the crown jewels? How did he get them? I was told that they were taken by the Karnivans."

Martha shook her head. "I saw what was about to happen, so I secreted the jewels just before the battle for Barrington. When your father was taken to Xanterra, I slipped them into his cell."

Eristan frowned. "Then where are they now?"

A perplexed look crossed the face of the old woman. "I don't know. Your father must have hidden them in his cell."

Eristan turned to his bodyguard. "Have Captain Trevarr send six of his most trusted men back to Xanterra to search my father's cell for the jewels."

"Aye, sire."

Princess Cordelia was ushered into the tent at that moment. She hurried to Eristan's side. "Eristan, what is going on? Lord Wallace came to my chambers and told me that an event of great family significance had taken place and that I was to go to you immediately. The royal coach was waiting just outside my door and I came as fast as possible. Eristan, what's wrong?"

Eristan took a deep breath. "Actually, Princess, it's good news—though it will come as quite a shock. Prepare yourself. All of our lives we have been told that King William was killed in the battle for Barrington Castle. He wasn't. Cordelia, our father is still alive."

Cordelia's gaze immediately darted to King William, who was now sitting up and staring into space. "Our father . . . ?" Her voice faltered, and she began to tremble. "Eristan, is this our father?"

Eristan nodded. "His mind is gone, Cordelia, and he doesn't know us, but this is our father."

Tears flooded Princess Cordelia's eyes as she knelt before her father and took both of his emaciated hands in hers. "Oh, Father," she sobbed. "Father, Father." With tears streaming down her cheeks she hugged him, holding his grizzled head against her shoulder and gently rocking back and forth. "Oh, Father."

She leaned away from him and looked into his face. "Father, don't you know me? I'm your daughter! I'm Cordelia!"

The eyes were blank and staring; the bearded face was expressionless.

Shaking with sobs, Cordelia looked at her brother. "He doesn't know me, Eristan. He doesn't even know me!"

Eristan knelt beside her and put an arm around her shoulders. He gently stroked her hair. "His mind is gone," he said hoarsely. "He hasn't spoken in years."

Overcome with emotion, the princess pulled away and rose to her feet. "Oh, Eristan, I can't bear to see him like this!" She took a deep breath and dabbed at her eyes. "I'm going outside."

"Cordelia?" The voice was hoarse and gravelly. "My little Cordelia?"

Cordelia spun around. "Father?"

"Don't leave me, Cordelia."

With a shriek of joy the princess dropped to her knees and threw her arms around her father. The tears started anew. "Oh, Father, do you know me? I'm Cordelia. I'm your daughter. Father, do you know me?"

Thin hands grabbed the princess by the shoulders, but their grip was firm as the elderly king held his daughter at arms' length. "Cordelia, is that really you? Where have you been, my little Sweetheart?"

The eyes were clear and focused and the bearded face was contorted with emotion. "Oh, Cordelia. My little Sweetheart."

Cordelia was sobbing so that she could scarcely speak. "I'm here, Father."

"And where is Eristan?"

"I'm right here, Father." King Eristan seized his father and crushed him against his chest in an enthusiastic hug.

William placed trembling hands on their shoulders and looked repeatedly from one to another. "My children, my children," he said quietly, and his eyes filled with tears. "Oh, Eristan, Cordelia, is it really you? For years I have thought that you were dead. First I lost your mother, and then I lost you."

An owl hooted in the darkness as King Eristan and King William finished a late night meal. "So that's how things stand in Cheswold, Father," Eristan said, as he concluded a lengthy narrative of the latest chapter in Cheswoldian history. "Vladimir was killed, and the two errant captains have sworn their allegiance to the throne and to Cheswold. Grimlor and the Karnivans are now preparing to invade Cheswold, perhaps even tomorrow."

He paused for a moment to stroke his father's wizened hand. "Father, I am told that you were a brilliant battle strategist. You're known as the 'Lion of Cheswold.' How would you defend Cheswold against the Karnivans?"

William took a deep breath. His voice was weak as he replied, "Son, don't fight the Karnivans."

Eristan was stunned. "What do you mean? Father, they're preparing to invade Cheswold!"

"Don't fight the Karnivans," the old man repeated. "Fight Grimlor."

"Father, you speak in riddles."

"The Karnivans have always been a peaceful, gentle people," William explained. "For generations they have been our staunchest allies and we have always worked together."

Eristan was perplexed. "What changed all that?"

"Grimlor. When Grimlor took the throne, he immediately began to put evil, bloodthirsty men in power. He built a powerful army and began to attack his neighbors. Not just Cheswold, but also Judenlan, Carpia, and Ainranon. Son, I firmly believe that if Grimlor were removed from the throne, Karniva would once again become a land of peace."

"What should we do?"

"Advise your captains that in the coming battle they are to seek to locate Grimlor and destroy him. Once Grimlor is out of the picture, Karniva will become a different neighbor."

"How shall I order the battle? Captains Orwyn and Vance want to cross the border and engage the Karnivans before they attack us."

The old man shook his head. "Grimlor has a powerful cavalry and he would crush your infantry like a man stepping on a worm. You need to find a way to engage him on your own terms and negate the advantage of his superior cavalry."

"How would we do that?"

William hobbled to the tent door and gazed out for a moment. "If my memory serves me correctly, five or six miles southwest of here lies Riffendor Swamp, which extends for three or four furlongs in both directions. It's a foul, muddy bog with standing water a foot or two deep. Have your men fell hundreds of trees and cut them into logs, then cast them into the swamp. Your infantrymen will then be able to outmaneuver Grimlor's cavalrymen.

"Build log rafts for your archers and place them at strategic points in the swamp. If you can engage Grimlor at Riffendor Swamp, his powerful cavalry will become a liability to him, rather than an asset." Taking a bit of charcoal, William quickly sketched a diagram of the swamp. "Place your squads of archers here, and here, and here and here. These are the points from which they can be most effective." He handed the parchment to Eristan.

"I would also suggest using karwac root to panic Grimlor's horses and create pandemonium in his ranks."

"How would we use karwac root?"

"When lighted, it explodes with an incredible amount of noise. The sound will spook the horses." He grinned. "Just be sure not to use it too close to your own cavalry."

Eristan laughed.

"And remember, your objective is not to destroy the Karnivan army, but to find and destroy Grimlor himself. Once that tyrant is out of the picture, Cheswold and Karniva can once again become allies, rather than enemies."

King Eristan embraced King William. "Father, it's so good to have you back."

The old man returned the embrace. "Son, you cannot imagine what joy it brings me to see what a fine man you have become. Lead your men against Grimlor and Karniva, but remember that victory will come as you put your trust in King Emmanuel. Ultimately, the battle is in his hands and victory must come from him."

For more than an hour, King Eristan and his father discussed battle strategies and plans for the confrontation with Grimlor and the Karnivans. Eristan's heart was full as he reveled in the presence of King William, the father he had never known. "What an honor it is to be your son," he said warmly. "Father, you were known as one of the greatest kings in Cheswold's history!"

King William seemed surprised, almost disappointed, at Eristan's words. A sober look crossed his countenance. "Nay, I was not great, Son," he replied slowly, almost sadly. "I loved my people, and I was their servant. I would rather be remembered as the servant of Cheswold."

The words struck Eristan's heart like a knife and he flinched, as if in pain. His father noticed. "What is it, Eristan?"

Eristan sighed deeply. "I have not been a servant to the people, Father. Following Lord Aric's advice, I have sought to be great, to be honored and lauded by my people." Tearfully, he told of the golden statues, portraits, and other ventures he had taken to advance his own glory. "I raised taxes to pay for all this," he admitted painfully, "though my people struggle just to exist. In truth, I have lived for myself and not for my people."

"King Emmanuel was the greatest servant of all," William said softly.

Eristan nodded. "As soon as the battle is over I shall give the orders to halt production of the portraits of me. The golden statue shall be melted down, and the people's taxes shall be lowered immediately. And Barrington Castle shall be open to all, rich and poor alike." He shook his head ruefully. "Father, how could I have been so foolish?"

William smiled. "King Emmanuel will be pleased with your new decisions."

Eristan nodded. "That is what I desire more than anything."

A racking cough shook William's slender body. He smiled feebly at Eristan. "If you don't mind, Son, I need to get a little rest."

"I'm sorry, Father, I didn't realize how late it was getting. I should have let you get to bed an hour ago." Eristan stood. "Good night, Father. Thank you for the battle strategy, and especially, for the example you set for me as a servant."

William smiled. "May Emmanuel grant you victory as you go against Grimlor."

King Eristan and his father sat side by side on a hillock overlooking Riffendor Swamp. Eristan knew that his father was dying, yet King William had insisted on being present for the battle against Grimlor. Together they watched the hordes of the Karnivan cavalry charge into the swamp in pursuit of the Cheswoldian infantry. "This battle is yours, Father," Eristan said quietly. "The Lion of Cheswold roars in battle once again!"

William coughed weakly. "May King Emmanuel smile upon Cheswold today," he replied. "Without his intervention, Cheswold is lost. Grimlor's armies are simply too powerful."

Wearing only hauberks and helmets, the men of Cheswold had cast off their lower body armor in order to be limber and light-footed. Leaping nimbly from log to log, they fought like wildcats, cutting, slashing and thrusting, and then leaping into the shallow waters so quickly that the enemy could not follow.

Karniva's powerful warhorses, heavy in body and limb, were slow and cumbersome in such a battle and could not maneuver as readily as the infantrymen. Thus, Grimlor lost his advantage in the battle for Riffendor Swamp.

"Your Majesty," an excited voice cried right beside Cheswold's two kings, "unless I am mistaken, that's Grimlor himself! There, sire—the big knight on the dappled gray stallion! The one swinging the mace, sire. What are your orders, sire?"

William turned to the captain. "Take your battalion and flank him at once," he ordered. "Get behind him to cut off any avenue of escape and then drive him within range of the archers. Once Grimlor is dead, the battle is over!"

"Aye, sire," came the eager reply. "At once, sire!" The captain turned to give the order.

At that moment, Garven led the Cheswoldian cavalry into the fray. The nimble Berkshire horses, smaller and lighter of limb than Grimlor's massive warhorses, actually had the advantage in the swamp battle, as they could maneuver easier. Garven's men managed to surround Grimlor's unit, and they battled furiously as they endeavored to penetrate the Karnivan king's defenses and do battle with him personally. Realizing what was about to take place, Grimlor wheeled his massive warhorse and fled.

As William and Eristan watched, Garven and his men gave chase. The smaller Cheswoldian horses quickly overtook the massive Karnivan warhorses. Surrounded by Cheswold's knights, Grimlor stood in the stirrups, turned, and swung his mace with all his strength. The deadly weapon caught Garven full in the helmet and he fell from the saddle with a scream of agony. Rage flooded through Eristan's soul as Garven's men fell back. Grimlor's stallion reached the bank and disappeared into the brush.

Infantrymen with smoldering torches began to light pieces of karwac root and fling them into the heaviest concentrations of Karnivan cavalry. The resulting explosions caused pandemonium among Grimlor's mounted troops. Powerful warhorses reared in terror at the horrific sounds, hurling their riders headlong into the swamp and causing many to strike their heads against the floating logs. Only after more than half the cavalry was out of the picture did the Karnivan captain sound the retreat.

With blood pouring from his helmet Garven leaped to his feet and cried mightily, "Men of Cheswold, Grimlor must not get away! After him! For King Eristan! For Cheswold!" The sturdy Berkshire horses raced across the swamp and swept up the bank, riding hard in pursuit of Grimlor.

King William turned to his son. "If Grimlor escapes, it matters not who wins the battle for the swamp. Eristan, your men must take Grimlor! They must!"

At that moment Grimlor and a handful of Karnivans swept into view, hotly pursued by a determined band of Cheswoldian knights. Water flew everywhere as Grimlor's huge stallion splashed into the swamp. Riding furiously, one of Cheswold's knights flanked Grimlor. He stood in the stirrups and leaped from his horse, knocking the Karnivan king from the saddle and bearing him into the mud of the swamp. In an instant, a dozen of Cheswold's knights leaped from their horses, surrounded Grimlor, and ended his life.

A knight lit a large piece of karwac root and hurled it high into the air. The resulting explosion rocked the valley, causing Karnivans and Cheswoldians alike to pause for an instant. "Men of Karniva, the battle is over!" the knight cried mightily. "Grimlor is dead!"

An unearthly silence settled across the swampy battlefield

for a long moment, and then a raucous cheer leaped from the throats of a thousand men. To Eristan's amazement, the Karnivan knights began leaping up and down and waving their weapons in the air as if to celebrate. Vile swamp water flew everywhere.

Eristan turned to his father. "Do the Karnivans not understand? Their king is dead! They just lost the battle! They act as if they are celebrating."

The cheering continued.

"Grimlor was a tyrant," his father answered soberly, "who held the gentle people of Karniva in bondage for all these years. Now at last they are free! Why should they not celebrate?"

"The mighty Lion of Cheswold has won a great victory," Eristan exulted, clapping a hand on his father's shoulder. "It was glorious to go into battle with you, Father."

"King Emmanuel won the victory for Cheswold," William said sternly, "not I. May the glory go to him."

Eristan nodded meekly.

William bent over in a prolonged spell of coughing and Eristan watched in alarm as the frail, wasted body was racked with pain. "I don't have many days left, Son. Soon King Emmanuel will call me to the Golden City." The old king took a deep, wheezing breath. "I want to see Barrington Castle before I die; I want to see my people. One hope kept me alive all these fourteen long years—the dream that I would one day return to Barrington and die among my people."

"And so it shall be," King Eristan declared, as a huge lump formed in his throat. "The royal carriage shall start for Barrington this very afternoon."

King William and King Eristan watched as a throng of Karnivan knights approached, leading several of their own captains in chains. "Grimlor's men," William said soberly. "The

Karnivans are surrendering them to you."

Eristan exhaled slowly. "The battle is over. Cheswold is saved."

"This is indeed a great day for Cheswold," William said quietly. "The people of Karniva shall once again be our neighbors, and the people of Cheswold shall be at peace."

Eristan nodded. "Aye, Father. And I shall be their servant."

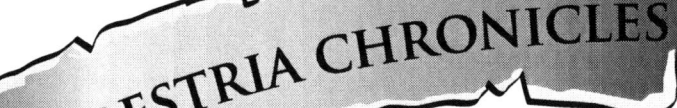

THE TERRESTRIA CHRONICLES

Have you read the companion series, The Terrestria Chronicles?

Want to share them with your friends?

The Sword, the Ring, and the Parchment

The Quest for Seven Castles

The Search for Everyman

The Crown of Kuros

The Dragon's Egg

The Golden Lamps

The Great War

All volumes available at

WWW.TALESOFCASTLES.COM